TOO MUCH BLOOD
IN THE HOSPITAL!

It was five minutes to eleven when Lance pulled into the nurses' parking lot and ran into the hospital through the front door. He turned right and there were several people, nurses, aides, an orderly and a tall man, standing in and around the kitchen doors.

Mrs. Collins' neat kitchen was a gory mess. The rich, ripe smell of blood was in the air. Blood had been poured over the work tables, the range, and the racks of dishes. Blood had been slung onto the walls. It pooled on the otherwise spotless floor. Food supplies, flour, salt, sugar, and rice had been poured atop the counters and mixed with blood.

"I'm gonna quit running errands around this place," nurse Scoggins said. "First I walk up and find a dead body, and then this!"

Also by Hugh Zachary:

BLOODRUSH

A CRIME COURT MYSTERY

MURDER IN WHITE

HUGH ZACHARY

Book Margins, Inc.

A BMI Edition

Published by special arrangement with Dorchester
Publishing Co., Inc.

If you purchased this book without a cover you should be aware
that this book is stolen property. It was reported as "unsold and
destroyed" to the publisher and neither the author nor the publisher
has received any payment for this "stripped book."

Copyright © MCMLXXXI by Hugh Zachary

All rights reserved. No part of this book may be reproduced or
transmitted in any form or by any electronic or mechanical means,
including photocopying, recording or by any information storage
and retrieval system, without the written permission of the Publisher,
except where permitted by law.

Printed in the United States of America.

Chapter One

On an August Friday with the Bermuda high pumping moist tropical air inland across the beaches of the Long Bay, that long sweep of shoreline curving inward from the Cape of Fear to Charleston, Marian Powers checked herself into Bellamy Memorial Hospital because she had found over the seventy-two years of her life that breathing is a rewarding experience.

The attack of acute bronchial asthma hit Miss Powers while she was strolling along the strand a hundred yards from the beach cottage she had recently purchased as both an investment and a personal extravagance. Not that she couldn't afford extravagances. She was, without doubt, the richest woman in Clarendon County, the beach cottage being only a minor asset among her real estate holdings which included the last large tract of wooded land suitable for development within several miles of the thriving little village of Earlysburg.

When she had the early warning of an attack, she increased her pace, slowing to mount the wooden steps leading from the strand to the cypress walkway which connected with the screened porch of the cottage. Inside, with her breathing becoming more and more labored, she carefully closed the windows, leaving the shoreside windows cracked for ventilation against the swift attacks of mildew to which beach cottages are prone.

She was gasping audibly when she went down the front stairs into the garage underneath the cottage. She drove with her usual care, not breaking any laws, across the causeway and the high bridge. When she reached Bellamy Hospital she was beginning to become alarmed and she allowed herself one liberty. Since the parking space in front of the hospital was taken up, she left her car in the nurses' parking lot. It could be moved later. She was seeing white spots in front of her eyes and her chest was wheezing. Her small and withered breasts heaved with the effort to force air into her starving system.

She sat down weakly at the admissions desk. Although she was an old and valued patient she did not recognize the young girl at the desk. She explained her problem between gasps. She was subjected to questions. Yes, she had adequate hospitalization insurance. No, there was no one other than herself to sign the release forms and the insurance forms and the financial responsibility forms. She fought her growing impatience and signed the papers.

"All right, Mrs. Powers," young Janice Blake said, popping her bubble gum with bored relish, "we'll just have an orderly get a wheel chair and take you back to the 'mergency room."

"It's Miss Powers," Marian said. "And that won't do. Just get Dr. Epstein, please. He'll know what to do."

"I'm afraid he's not in the hospital," Janice said.

"Then we can have a nurse do it. I know well

enough from experience what is necessary. I'll need an immediate injection of one to one thousand epinephrine, a zero-point-three cc dose."

"Gee, you sound like a doctor," Janice said, not convinced.

"I am not a doctor," Marian said firmly. "Now will you please just assign me a private room and send a nurse to me immediately?"

"Gee, I dunno," Janice said. She looked over her shoulder. The administrator was not in her office. "Ruth," she yelled at the receptionist-telephone operator, "is Dr. King in the hospital yet?" Meanwhile she was pulling out Miss Powers' records. She was, indeed, a regular customer.

"He's down in emergency," the receptionist called back.

"All right, Miss Powers," Janice said. "We'll put you in room two."

An orderly arrived with a wheel chair. The world threatened to go all gray as Marian was pushed down the hall, past the nurse's station, around the corner. An LPN followed the chair and started fussing with the bed.

"Please get out of the way," Marian said, half-falling onto the bed, bundling the pillow to raise her head.

It was just before three o'clock in the afternoon. Dr. John King was in room two within five minutes. Marian had seen him before. He was one of the weekend doctors. He was tall, a bit on the slim side, silvered at the temples in spite of his youth. There was a hint of something, character, soul, suffering, in his gray eyes.

"My records," Marian gasped, thrusting her purse at him.

King opened the purse, found the packet of records. "Yes," he said. "I see." He sent the LPN away and she returned with an ampule of epinephrine. King checked the label and injected .3 cc and within minutes Marian was breathing again. The transformation was almost miraculous.

"I allowed myself too much time in the sun," she explained. "I'm so sorry to have troubled you."

"Since your condition is chronic, you should carry a preparation with you," Dr. King said.

"It's one of my weaknesses," Marian said. "The idea of sticking a needle into myself is abhorrent to me."

Dr. King, following the procedures outlined in Marian's medical records, left orders for hourly injections. He went back to the emergency room to finish flushing out an elderly man with locked bowels. As he stood and turned away from the bed Marian saw that he had terrible scars on the back and side of his neck.

She tried to sleep as the noisy business of the hospital went on around her. Nurses congregated outside her door to gossip. Orderlies banged things. Visitors opened and closed her door by mistake or out of curiosity. She thought about the cottage and decided that she was not sorry she had bought it. It had been a distress sale and she could make a good profit any time she wanted to sell. However, she would, she decided, keep the cottage, rent it during the summer, and move into it for a few weeks in late September and October when the beach was truly lovely. There was always the problem of being ten miles away from the hospital, but she'd make it through this attack successfully, and in the event of a real emergency there was quite an efficient rescue squad on the beach. She had contributed money to it.

Breathing easily as the drug opened up the clogged air passages in her lungs, she felt fine. The asthma was her one affliction, and it was an old and familiar enemy. Aside from asthma she was as healthy as a horse, and each time she visited Dr. Epstein for a checkup he told her she would live to be a hundred and fifty. He was wrong, but she had no way of knowing it. She would live for just under twelve more hours.

The outside temperature at 3:30 p.m. was 88 degrees. Humidity was 84 percent. Winds on the Clarendon beaches were light, zero to 5 mph. The ocean was flat and dotted with small boats. Only a ripple of surf ran on to the dark sand where Lance Carver was playing hooky from his job. Fortier Beach was at its peak summer population, with all cottages filled with as many people as there were beds. The main highway running the length of the island was abuzz with traffic.

Lance had picked his spot on the far eastern end of the island where ocean front lots sold for six hundred dollars per front foot, and the expense of the real estate, consisting of high sand dunes, had slowed development, leaving vacant lots between cottages which offered good access to the strand. His Sheriff's Department black and white car was parked on a strip of cement which was all that remained of a cottage destroyed in the hurricane of 1954. The car's windows were down to help prevent the buildup of heat from the August sun. Lance had picked his time and slipped into his swim trunks in the front seat. He lay on a GI blanket, just above the high tide line. The strand in front of him was marred by the salt-blackened and waterlogged stumps of an ancient cypress forest.

The eastern end of the beach was relatively private. Local people used it for picnics and sunbathing. There was, of course, no lifeguard on duty as there was at the public beach, but neither were there hundreds of upstate people trying to cram a whole summer of beaching into one week or one day.

The sun felt good on his skin. He oozed perspiration, but was cooled by the very slight southeast breeze. He had his shirt lying loosely over his left shoulder where the scar was still sensitive to the sun. His eyes were comfortable behind a wide pair of sunglasses. He would do precious little tanning, and didn't need it since his skin had a permanent tan lightened only by the usual trace of white blood found in most American blacks. He had allowed himself one cold beer from the six-pack cooler in the trunk. Now the beer was gone and he had just thirty minutes to get back to town to pick up Miss Annie Mae Duncan and give her a ride down to Spook Swain's office.

He dressed in the car, pulling his uniform pants over the dry trunks. Miss Annie Mae lived next door to him. She was waiting, dressed in a long black dress, carrying a huge pocketbook. She was, understandably, resentful and agitated.

"You de law, Lance," she said. "An' that's the natural truth, an' de law says I's got to go with you—"

"Miss Annie Mae, the law doesn't say I have to give you a ride," Lance said. "And listen, all you have to do is promise to pay. You understand that?

All you got to do is promise."

"I done done that. I promised. I pay when I can."

It was one of the more unpleasant parts of his job, this, serving the papers when someone got behind in his bills. And a local merchant paid good money to have the Sheriff's Department drag some citizen into the magistrate's office.

Since it was late in the day Spook's office was empty. Lance stood aside and let Miss Annie Mae walk in and have a seat in one of the metal chairs. He nodded to Spook.

"The complaining merchant is a little late, Deputy," Spook said.

"That's all right," Miss Annie Mae said. "You took me 'way from my kitchen. All I got to do is wait."

"Mr. Swain," Lance said. You didn't call Spook by his nickname in his own office. "Since the complaining merchant is not present, perhaps Miss Annie Mae could just go home? She has assured me that she will pay when she can."

Magistrate Swain was dressed in a neat gray suit. His white shirt was spotless. His hair was full and waved into a field of whiteness. He looked, Lance thought, like a magistrate, cool, dignified. He could be severe. Lance did a lot of business with Spook. At first, when Spook was first appointed magistrate by the District Superior Court Judge, the brothers had rejoiced, and when they were in minor trouble they tried to get sent up to Spook's office instead of the office of the other magistrate, an old-timer with white skin. The brothers soon discovered that they usually fared better, if they were guilty, with the white magistrate. Spook believed in dignity, not only for himself, but for his race. He had very little patience with a brother who had deliberately done wrong and usually slapped on the stiffer fines.

The complaining merchant arrived just as Spook was about to release Miss Annie Mae with a lecture and a caution to pay the bill. The merchant had the charge slip for an electric toaster. The balance due was ten dollars and it was six months past due.

"I had a sickness," Miss Annie Mae explained.

"But you have Medicare, Annie Mae," the merchant said.

"I lost two months work," Miss Annie Mae said. "I back at work now. I got a week's pay comin'. I pay you two dollars on Monday."

"Mr. Swain—" the merchant appealed to Spook.

"Could you pay a little more than two dollars?" Spook asked, in a kind voice. "It has been a long time."

Miss Annie Mae stiffened. "I say I pay two dollars. That's all I can pay. I pay two dollars Monday and two dollars the next Monday and on like that."

"Perhaps she could go to the welfare," the merchant suggested.

Miss Annie Mae bristled. "I ain't never had to take no welfare yet, and I ain't startin' now."

The merchant looked at her with disbelief. "Annie Mae, you'd qualify. Your age. Your income. Food stamps, at least."

"I been feedin' myself for seventy-one years," Annie Mae said. "I got my old age money, but I figure I worked for that. I stay well, I pays my bills, and I pays 'em now, just a little slow."

Spook cleared his throat. "I think, in view of the facts, that a payment of two dollars per week would be adequate."

"I thank you," Miss Annie Mae said, standing.

"I'll give you a ride home," Lance said.

"I can walk," Miss Annie Mae said angrily.

"No need for that," Lance said, following her out.

"You jest go 'way and leave me be, Lance Carver," she said, moving her old body draped in long clothing down the stairs with surprising agility. "You de law, goin' 'round pickin' on old ladies."

Lance stopped at the top of the stairs. The white merchant came up behind him. "Hate to do that," he said.

"Ummm," Lance said.

"Cost me almost as much as she owed to take the papers."

Lance knew how much it cost.

"Can't let 'em get out in front of you, though," the merchant said. "Have to take out papers now and then to show 'em you mean business."

"Yeah," Lance said.

"I could have asked Mr. Swain to make her pay court costs, you know."

"Yeah, you're all heart," Lance said, moving across in front to go down the stairs.

Miss Annie Mae was swishing her long skirt down main street. Lance honked and waved and she put her nose in the air. It was quitting time. He drove into the black section of town and parked the county cruiser on what was left of the grass in front of his three room shotgun house. Although he'd left the house open, it was steamy hot. He made a pitcher of tea and pulled off his shirt. With a tall glass of iced tea in his right hand he walked into the bedroom and looked at the shoulder in the mirror. The small, star-shaped scar in front was not too noticeable. When he turned, looking at his back, the exit scar was a large, irregular welt. They had told him they could fix it, do some repair, but he'd said, "What the hell difference does it make?"

He sat on the edge of the bed and for a moment he could smell her, Glenda, some lingering fragrance, some tiny remnant of femininity in the room. He put the iced tea on the bedside table and fell back, still in his shoes and uniform pants. When you let some crazy kill your wife, how important is a scar on your shoulder?

Chapter Two

Someone has blown it, Jug Watson was thinking. It's as simple as that, someone had blown it, underestimating the emotional factors involved.

Jug was running for reelection and it should have been simple. He had counted on spending a minimum of time running around the county at the wheel of his personal black and white, Clarendon County Sheriff's Department Unit One. In spite of the fact that the car had spent most of the week in the county garage the air conditioner sounded like two tom cats caught in a cement mixer and spewed hot air which smelled of burning rubber. Jug was working the outskirts of Swansey, up on Highway 17, stopping at the country service stations and general stores to press a little flesh and remind anyone who would listen that he wanted to work for the county for one more four year term.

At sixty-four, Jug needed another term as sheriff like he needed to try to sandpaper a tiger's twat, but what was he to do when the only man who wanted the job was Chief Deputy Dennis Watts?

Between stops Jug thought a lot about the hammock he and Bessie had put up under the two trees in the back yard where the demented whippoorwill called Valentino spent his evenings yowling his head off. He thought also about the need to weed his garden, but then he'd also think about the gaggle of smart-assed young lawyers who had the audacity to put up a primary opponent against him. That hadn't happened since the first time he ran for the office, more years past than he liked to remember.

The young lawyers didn't have a chance to beat him, not with a kid fresh out of the Army, a kid whose only law enforcement experience had been as a military policeman at Ft. Bragg. Clarendon was Jug Watson's county. He knew it from Green Swamp to Ocean, from the South Carolina line to the outskirts of the metro sprawl of New Hanover County. He knew the woods and how to find a deer when no one else could, and he didn't like the fact that the county was changing, growing, edging reluctantly into the twentieth century with industrial growth and tourism and the building of cottages along the beaches. He had been sheriff in Clarendon when most of the county was either swamp or slash pine pulp forests and, tired as he was, he intended to be sheriff for four more years, just to help as best he could in the growing pains.

Jug began his campaign in July. He began with the usual confidence. He had the kind of memory which is gold to policemen and politicians, remembering first, middle, and last names of thousands, knowing in most cases the family history and the names of the children and sometimes the dogs. So he was not pleasantly surprised to run into some resentment out in the country, away from the county seat, where people were talking more about the county hospital than about Jug Watson running for sheriff again.

Those damned young lawyers again.

They'd pushed through a bond issue in the last election to put up a new hospital. Now they were agitating among the out-county folk to insist on a more central location. Since central location in

Clarendon would have put the hospital in three feet of water in the middle of the Green Swamp, the young lawyers were talking about a location closer to Swansey and the citizens of Earlysburg and Fortier Beach, on the eastern end of the county, were dead set against moving the hospital out of Earlysburg. The resentments being built up were rubbing off on Jug. He didn't like that a bit.

Earlysburg faced the Cape Fear with houses built before the American Revolution. Stable populatation was around three thousand, swelling a bit in the summer. It had been county seat of Clarendon since the days when Indians still had oyster feasts on the unsettled beaches, when Swansey was a family fish camp. Naturally, all government buildings, except for the new jail in Swansey, were concentrated in Earlysburg. Swansey was nothing more than an upstart, although it could boast, now, of almost equal population. The town had grown willy-nilly on either side of the main north to south tourist route, and the oldest buildings there dated back to the 1930's. To the old timers of Earlysburg, the Swansey people were almost as alien as the New Jersey Yankees who stopped in Swansey to gas up and buy a pint for the road in the state controlled liquor store.

The problem was, Jug knew, that the western end of the county held the power. Get everyone together outside Earlysburg and Fortier Beach and the east end of the county could be overwhelmed. Jug was not about to see his long stint as sheriff end before he wanted it to end just because he lived in Fortier Beach and had his office in the county seat. He tried to dodge the hospital issue and when he couldn't he suggested a compromise, a site somewhere between Swansey and Earlysburg.

"My daddy farmed right out in that area," he would say. "I grew up running between both towns." He didn't mention that in those days Swansey was nothing more than a fish house and a service station. "I didn't move to the east until I was elected sheriff so's I could be near the office. You folks have your own deputies live right here in your area. They work with you and look after you, and I want you to remember it was Jug Watson set up that system of spreading the deputies out over the county. The sheriff's office is not an Earlysburg office, it's a Clarendon office, and it just happens to be located in the county seat."

He'd win, but the kid would get a few thousand protest votes because of the hospital issue. Then it would be over and all he'd have lost was a bit of his pride, because the Republicans, as usual, had not put up a candidate. In Clarendon, if two Republican votes were counted in the same precinct they were both thrown out because everyone knew that rascal had voted twice.

Jug ate a barbecue sandwich at Harrel's Crossroads and developed gas. He called it a day and drove back east, passed the hospital, looking at it bitterly. It was a sturdy, red brick building and it looked fine to him. He didn't approve of spending money on a new hospital. The United States was the only country in the world which tore down perfectly good buildings just because they were fifty years old. He'd been in Bellamy Memorial during the winter for a GI series and other tests, and he didn't see a thing wrong with it.

Passing the two beer-joints which faced each other across the road into town he checked them out. They were inside the city and the primary responsibility of the Earlysburg police, but Clarendon was a large county, thinly populated, and the two municipal forces worked closely with the sheriff's office, the sheriff's office handling all radio communications at night, exchanging favors, covering for each other when men were spread thin, as they always were.

It was the time of day for the small boats to start coming in from the shoals. Jug drove down past the boat harbor and parked to let the southeast breeze blow in the window. He watched as an outboard was pulled from the water up the ramp on to a trailer. The cleaning tables were all in use, the catch being mostly bluefish. Down in front of the shed he could see Burt Scoggins bending under the bottom of a charter fisherman, using a bristle brush and sand to scrub the barnacles and slime from the wooden hull.

Burt was a small man. His chin fell away from his mouth all the way to his adam's apple, and when he was concentrating he swallowed continuously, adam's apple moving on a ten-mile trip each time before coming to rest. Burt was serving a thirty-day sentence one weekend at a time. It wasn't his first sentence for public drunkenness. Jug or the Earlysburg police had carried Burt into the recorder's court many times, but the last time when Jug took him in Burt showed that he had a conscience.

"Your honor," Burt said to the judge, his adam's apple working furiously, "I do just fine through the week, but I jest cain't stand them Saturday nights."

Burt did work hard from seven-thirty Monday morning until five on Friday, but by ten o'clock on a Friday night the devil tilted the world under him. Meantime, his wife, Betty Mae, was working as a practical nurse—Burt liked to use the jargon and call her an LPN—or she was at home with the four of her five children who still lived with them, and all the time she was hoping that Burt would make it through Saturday with at least some of his paycheck.

Jug wasn't worried about Burt's vote. He had Burt's vote on a permanent basis because he'd always looked after Burt when things got too blurred and bleary, giving him the sleeping cell. It was Betty Mae's vote which concerned Jug when he took Burt into the recorder's court the last time. Her vote, of course, was just one vote, but she was a woman and women had a way of sticking together. Betty Mae was a small, rounded woman with a cheerful smile and she was well liked. Jug knew that if he and the judge put Burt away for thirty days there'd be hell to pay. Betty Mae would tell everyone she knew that they'd taken her man away from her and deprived her of his paycheck just because he was doing what he seemed to do best. Jug had seen it happen before when the arresting officer and the judge got the blame for the jailing and not the defendant. And even though the judge was not up for election he didn't want all of Betty Mae's friends mad at him.

"What do you think, Jug?" the judge asked, looking at his watch. The summer run of bluefish had just started.

"Well, Judge," Jug said. "There's this new work release program, and Burt could spend the nights here in the jail, but that wouldn't solve it, because a man's got to see his younguns sometimes when he has as many as Burt here has."

"They could visit," the judge said, thinking about the tide and the hungry bluefish.

"Jail's no place for kids," Burt said, lifting his almost nonexistent chins.

"Or," Jug said, "we could, since it's the weekends that throw Burt, just lock him up on weekends."

It worked beautifully. Betty Mae would come by the jail on Friday evening with a fresh change of clothing for Burt, pick up his paycheck and hang around to see if Dodo Walser was feeding Burt right. Betty Mae liked it because she was getting all of Burt's paycheck to catch up on bills. Jug liked it because Burt wasn't out on the Saturday night streets playing God's Own Drunk and the only one to complain was Dodo. After all, the jail was almost like Dodo's home. He'd been jailer there forever. He mowed the grass in the small area between the old brick building and the chainlink fence and raked the leaves under the huge oaks. He kept the floor swabbed and reputtied the windows every ten years or so when the winds off the river began to make the panes rattle. Dodo, as his name implied, was not the intellectual giant. He was still trying to figure out a joke from years past when some college kid got a lot of laughs with a button which read Intellectuals For Wallace, but he knew his job and he did it well. In return, the county paid him a salary and let him sleep in the front room and cook for himself and the occasional guest. Most of the prisoners were now sent to the new jail in Swansey, so the guest was usually Burt.

Dodo didn't mind having Burt for a guest when Burt was drunk. Then he'd be poured into the bunk and he wouldn't do more than groan until midday Sunday. Sober, Burt was something else. He was always wanting water or a cup of coffee and, probably because he was sober, he had nightmares which made Dodo's white hair stand on end.

Thirty days in weekends is a long time. Dodo didn't think that it seemed any longer to Burt than to him, however. It went on and on, and that Friday in August was just another weekend with Burt finishing up at the boat harbor and walking slowly up through town to the jail. Just another hot summer evening but with one important difference.

The day before, on Thursday, two of Jug's deputies had brought fifty half-gallon fruit jars of prime white lightning out of the Green Swamp. The man who owned the still was an old hunting buddy of Jug's and didn't hold the raid against him because Jug just happened to mention to a cousin who mentioned it to his cousin who passed it along that the revenue boys out of Raleigh had been tipped. All the deputies and the revenue agents brought out was the booze in half-gallen fruit jars. It swirled oily and white and rich and they poured all of it except two jars down the storm sewer at the corner next to the jail. All that pure white stuff ran down the storm sewer into the river and Pappy Crowder swore that the flounders in the river were so drunk that they didn't even feel a gig. Some of the boys had shrimp after making a drag in the river and they said the shrimp came out marinated like in a fancy French restaurant. It was potent stuff.

And Burt walked past the storm drain. It hadn't rained. The aroma didn't register immediately, it just lodged itself in Burt's subconscious mind and festered and woke him in the early evening. He had been dreaming about drinking a great big glass of prime white lightning, and that was strange because he'd given up drinking stump juice as soon as he began to make enough money to buy bonded bourbon. But he could taste it.

What had waked Burt, actually, was Dodo yelling at him to wake up and eat. The judge had caught bluefish that day and brought them around to the jail. With grits and fried cornpone it was fittin', but Burt did not eat. When he reached up to take his plate he looked over Dodo's shoulder and saw, up there on the high shelf the evidence from the raid into the swamp. He saw two half-gallon jars of pure white corn liquor. It hadn't settled down good from the ride out of the swamp. It was almost alive, swirling inside, reflecting the light in a tantalizing way.

"My God," Burt said. "My God, Dodo, what's that?"

"That's the evidence," Dodo said. "You gonna eat this or do I throw it to the dogs?"

Burt took the plate but he couldn't eat. His mouth was dry and he couldn't chew. His subconscious mind had absorbed the smell from the storm sewer. He couldn't keep his eyes off the evidence. He would take a bite and his tongue would swell into a hard knot and the bite would get bigger and bigger.

"Dodo," he said, when the old man came to take away the tray, "I don't feel so good."

In room two, lower floor, Bellamy Memorial Hospital, Marian Powers felt fine. She had enjoyed her dinner. The food was basic, but well seasoned. The nurse who worked the three to eleven shift had given her her eight o'clock injection of epinephrine. Marian had another seven hours to live.

Chapter Three

She would have been deeply shamed by her appearance. At first the light was dim, but when the light was dim there were no eyes to see her, her hair melted from customary neatness by the sweat and exertion of her final struggles, her lips gnawed and caked with dried blood, her staring eyes protruding slightly. And most shameful of all her body, trim for a lady of her age but sagged and wrinkled by time, her body which no man had seen totally naked—not even her doctors, since she always insisted on being draped carefully for examination—her body was exposed for all to see.

Her chin had fallen forward to rest above her small, loose breasts, her hair wet with sweat trailing down her cheeks. Her arms hung by her sides, her fingers just below the seat level of the receptionist's chair. She was held in place by a large band of rubber tubing which dug into the soft flesh under her breasts and was tied in a careful slipknot behind the chair's back. From the rear, she being a small woman, it would have looked—if anyone had chanced to look—as if someone had sat down to rest in the receptionist's chair. To her left, the short hall extended past the darkened business offices to the closed kitchen. To her right the swinging doors to the lower patient wing were closed. Beyond the doors the brightly lit nurses station was quiet. Delphi Pond, one year out of UNCW School of Nursing, was seated at the desk reading a nursing magazine. She was a small jewl of a girl, built with loving precision in near miniature: body perfect, face pretty enough to have turned in her twenty-four years quite a number of male heads. Mrs. Lowery, the senior RN on the eleven-to-seven graveyard shift, was seated across from the station on the couch, knitting a sweater for her baby granddaughter. Betty Mae Scoggins, LPN, had answered the bedpan call in room seven. When she returned she asked if anyone wanted coffee. Delphi said, "Sure, if you're fixing."

"I'm fixing, Miss Lazy," Betty Mae said.

Betty Mae was just an inch taller than Delphi, which made her, too, a short lady. But she was built along more generous lines, and giving birth to five children for Burt had put tear marks and extra padding on her stomach. She looked solid, dependable, a pillar of American womanhood on which is built, well, in her case, a family of seven presided over by a weekend drunk.

Betty Mae smiled. She smiled as a habit and as a rule. She smiled because she believed. She believed in the Lord, in herself, in her children—the oldest was on a football scholarship at East Carolina and would have gone to Chapel Hill if he'd had better grades—and, God help her, she even believed in Burt. She believed in the doctors at Bellamy Memorial and in the nursing staff, and when a patient was lost, like the poor little lady in room two, bless her, she believed that was the will of God.

Betty Mae also believed that a cup of coffee without sugar is not a cup of coffee, and the plastic cup of sugar was empty. "Drat," she said. "I'll have to go to the kitchen." But first she fixed Delphi's coffee, just cream and not much of it, and handed it to her. Then she bustled through the swinging door and down the hall leading to the receptionist's desk with the long corridor leading back to the emergency room and the labs and the empty waiting room in front and the darkened business offices on the right. She started to speak to the person who was resting in the receptionist's chair, someone, probably, who had walked up from emergency to find a place to sit down.

"Good Lord above," she said. Once, when she was a teenage girl, she had used profanity. "Oh, Lord," she said, in her rather naturally loud voice.

"Betty Mae?" Delphi called, coming to stand in the door.

"You and Lowery come here," Betty Mae said.

Lowery, at fifty-one, gray and regal in her whites, had done a stint at the South Carolina hospital for the insane. She'd seen it all. She had gone far past the capacity for shock in her years as a registered nurse, but there was still plenty of room for indignation. Delphi was still young enough to cry. She did it quietly.

They stood there, the three of them, all in white, the two RN's in their caps, standing close as if to draw comfort from each other.

"Oh, Lord Jesus," Betty Mae said, "she weren't dead. The poor, poor thing weren't dead. She went looking for help."

"She was dead," Mrs. Lowery said in a harsh voice. "I saw that she was dead, and Dr. King saw that she was dead and certified her as being dead."

"Then how?" Delphi asked.

"I don't know how," Mrs. Lowery said, "but someone does and that someone is in a whole heap of trouble." Her eyes were squinted. Lowery, angry, was a formidable force. Everyone in the hospital knew that. She'd been at Bellamy so long she owned the place, or so some said, or at least they said she acted as if she owned it. "Del, I want you to call Dr. Epstein."

"Yes ma'am." Delphi considered reaching around in front of Marian Powers to use the telephone on the switchboard but decided against it. She went back to the nurses station.

"Who in the world would do a thing like that?" Betty Mae asked.

"Who, indeed?" Lowery asked. Delphi came back.

"He's on his way."

"Betty Mae, I want you to stand right here and see that no one, I mean no one, comes in that front door," Lowery said, pushing Betty Mae past the desk into the waiting room. "And you, Delphi, do the same for the hall. If anyone comes up from emergency, stop them."

It was not necessary to tackle any intruder, although Betty Mae would have, for Dr. Ruben Epstein was the first person to enter the front door. It was almost dawn. Epstein looked as if he'd thrown himself together in more of a hurry than usual. Betty Mae, from long experience, made a necessary check. As usual Epstein's fly was unzipped. She made zipping motions, shaking her head. Epstein frowned, looked down, and muttered darkly as he closed the zipper. He was tall, with that type of handsome craggy face which is seen in old testament illustrations but without the beard. The habitual cigarette was hanging from his lips.

His voice was non-Southern, but it had been softened by his years in the South. "Well, Betty

Mae?" His hair was standing awry. Betty Mae stood aside and he walked through the opening beside the reception-telephone desk. He took the cigarette out of his mouth and blinked several times. When he spoke his voice was as usual calm almost cold.

"Why wasn't she picked up?" he asked.

"Bridge was on an ambulance run to New Hanover," Mrs. Lowery said. Bridge was Bridge Truval, undertaker and, by popular election, Clarendon County Coroner. "We've been expecting him at any time."

"It is not good policy," Epstein said. "You know my orders. When a patient dies, he is to be removed immediately."

"I couldn't carry her down on my back," Lowery said.

"Hummp," Epstein snorted. He bent to examine the length of rubber tubing which held Marian Powers in the chair.

"I don't see how they could get her past all three of us," Delphi said.

"Could have carried her out the back door and all the way around the front," Lowery said.

Epstein put a hand on his back, grunted, and straightened up. "Call Jug Watson."

"Do we have to?" Lowery asked. "With the whole county trying to close the hospital?"

"Better call," Epstein said. "Any coffee?"

Delphi got coffee. Epstein liked it black. While she was gone Lowery called Jug. It took Jug fifteen minutes to drive in from Fortier Beach with his lights going. It was beginning to lighten in the east, and the early fishermen were already up and about. Jug was a morning man, but not a predawn man.

He looked almost as loosely thrown together as Epstein. His voice was deep with morning phlegm. He asked slow questions and found out all there was to know.

"I'd like to move her back to the room," Epstein said.

"We really shouldn't," Jug said.

"Jug, you know what this hospital means to all of us, to the whole town," Epstein said.

"I know," Jug said. "And I'm with you. Not that I'd want my feelings broadcast out in the county right now."

"I'd hate to see some sick prankster make real problems for the hospital right now," Epstein said.

"Doc, this is Miss Marian Powers," Jug said.

"All the more reason," Epstein said. "I liked Miss Marian too well to submit her to this. Newspapers. People snickering about her being naked."

"She was a fine lady," Jug said.

"Now that she's dead everyone will soon know just how fine she was," Epstein said.

"How's that?"

"Miss Marian told me a couple of years ago when there was first talk about moving the hospital that she was going to leave the bulk of her estate to Bellamy Memorial," Epstein said.

Jug whistled. "Way I hear it most of her money is in land."

"Land can be sold or borrowed against," Epstein said.

"The bulk, huh? Any idea how much?"

"Aside from her asthma she was healthy for a seventy-two-year-old woman. Outlived all her relatives. I wasn't counting on anything from her for a number of years. I frankly have no idea. She may have left some to other charities and maybe a couple of friends. Over a million, though, I'd guess."

"Tell me again how she died," Jug said.

"She had a long history of violent asthma attacks. In spite of the fact that she checked out good just a couple of months ago, her heart was evidently weakened. She had a reaction to the drug which we've been using to treat her asthma. It was unfortunate, and it was unavoidable. We knew the danger was there when we used the drug, but she had always tolerated it well and it produced good results."

"Any way the hospital can be blamed for her death?"

"None."

"You weren't here when she died?" Jug asked.

"No. It happened so quickly. I was called, of course. She's my patient. But Dr. King was doing everything there was to be done. Once she went into the reaction she was dead within a few minutes. Dr. King certified her as being dead and I saw no reason to come out. I'd seen her during my evening rounds and she was feeling fine, good pulse, heart regular, strong and sassy and full of plans when she went home tomorrow—this morning."

"Exactly what will be listed as cause of death?" Jug asked.

"Cardiac arrest," Epstein said. "Preceeded by muscular tremor, dilatation, and fibrillation."

"I still call acid indigestion *heartburn*," Jug said. "She had a heart attack."

"Yes."

"Brought on by the drug?"

"Yes and no. What can I say? Without the drug she'd have died of asthma, or by heart failure brought on by lack of oxygen. The cause of death was asthma assisted by old age, but we'll go on record with cardiac arrest."

"I just want to be sure that no one can say that the medicine gave her the heart attack," Jug said. "You know people. A lot of them still say stay out of hospitals if they want to stay alive."

Epstein rewarded Jug with a frown of distaste. "A fatal reaction to epinephrine is always a faint possibility, but it usually takes a much larger dosage. The cases of fatalities which are on record have to do mostly with larger doses being administered by mistake."

"Any chance of that in Marian's case?" Jug asked.

"No. We were using ampules of the drug in the proper dosage. If she had been given an overdose it wouldn't have been an accident, but that sort of speculation is academic because she was not overdosed."

"Know that for sure, do you?" Jug asked.

"Not without autopsy, of course," Epstein dribbled cigarette ashes down his shirt and brushed them off without taking the butt from his lips. "But to give the minimum fatal dose for a healthy person someone would have had to pump ampule after ampule into her, and she wouldn't have stood still for that. She knows how much of the stuff she's supposed to get as well as we do."

"Doc, under the circumstances, just to protect yourself and the hospital, how do you feel about an autopsy?"

Epstein mused for a moment. "She wouldn't

like. She's always, because of her problem, had a great interest in medicine. She had arranged to donate her body to the Duke School of Medicine."

"I can order an autopsy," Jug said.

"Yes, I know. I guess you're right."

"People all over the county are talking about the hospital," Jug said. "They're going to say it's strange that Miss Marian died in the hospital just in time to give it a big sum of money to pull it through the crisis."

"They'll say it with or without an autopsy," Epstein said.

"But they won't have a leg to stand on if we do everything legal and thorough. I don't have to point out to you that they'd talk about you, you being chief of staff, and this hospital being, you might say, your life. I'm thinking of you as much as I am of the hospital."

"I appreciate that, Jug."

"Now the immediate question is why would someone pull a trick like taking off Miss Marian's gown and moving her out here into the hall? You got any ideas on that?"

"If this were a large training hospital I'd suspect high spirited medical students," Epstein said. "But in Bellamy? Your guess is as good as mine."

Jug was beginning to think about splurging with a breakfast down at the Marina Restaurant where the waffles were good and the maple syrup sickeningly sweet. "Doc, I guess the less fuss made about this the better."

"For the sake of the hospital, I'd agree," Epstein said.

"As it is, short of upsetting Betty Mae and the nurses, no harm done, is there?"

"No harm done."

"Might be a good idea to tell your people on the night shifts to keep their eyes open, maybe tighten up your security a little."

"What security?" Epstein asked, with a snort. "We have enough people on duty at night to do the job, but short of locking and bolting the doors there's no way we can keep an eye on the whole place. It's my opinion that someone in the hospital did it. In the early hours of the morning someone who knows this place could move around all over it without being seen."

"Well, I been in the business of keeping my eye on things for a lot of years," Jug said. "If you got some free time this afternoon you and me can get together and maybe come up with some suggestions about how to close up the place a little tighter at night."

Epstein used one of his rare smiles. It had the effects of a smirk. "The blues are running, Jug."

Jug grinned back. Epstein had a small boat and the reputation of being a little bit crazy. The charter boats would come up on him out in the blue water, his small craft falling completely out of sight in the troughs, all alone, hair blowing in the wind, two fishing rods in holders. "O.K., Doc. We'll just see what develops. Maybe our prankster will have had enough with this one."

The waffle was good and the syrup sweet and the restaurant was full of early risers, some of them voters, most of them summer people getting ready for fishing trips. Jug washed down the sweetness with three cups of coffee, knowing in advance that he'd pay with an acid stomach for his indulgence, shook a few hands and drove down into Jabbertown with the rising sun coming in the rear window. It was going to be another hot one. The black section of town was rising, with rock music coming from one set of open windows, Frank Adams trying to get a lawnmower started to do the grass in the cool of the morning, young kids already out with crab lines in their hands heading for the boat harbor.

Jug parked beside the department car in front of Lance Carver's house and waited a few minutes after his knock, hearing Lance stumbling around getting on his clothes. Lance's eyes were sleep-swollen and his hair mussed. He had on a uniform with the short sleeved shirt hanging out.

"Day's half over, boy," Jug said.

"Not before breakfast," Lance said, knowing that he was fighting a losing battle. He'd been trying to educate Jug not to call him boy for almost a year.

"When I get called up early everybody gets up," Jug said. "Got any coffee?"

Lance heated water for instant. Jug sat at the small table. The place had the look of a bachelor's house, not dirty but a bit dusty, a bit untidy, a musty smell. Jug waited until Lance had poured and sat down. "You got anything hot going?"

"Not much," Lance said. "Spook has some papers to serve Monday. I wanta talk to a couple of kids sometime this weekend about the vandalism at the high school."

"Your buddy, P.J. Charlie, still workin' at the hospital?"

"Less he got fired since yesterday."

"You look to me like you could use a nice restful night in the hospital," Jug said, blowing on the hot coffee.

"I had all the nights in the hospital I want," Lance said, feeling an urge to rub his shoulder and stopping his hand halfway up.

Jug told him about Miss Marian Powers. "I thought you'd be a good one to just hang around a little, out of uniform, see how the place runs, talk with your friend and some of the nurses, just get an idea about who has free run of the place at night, and see if anyone has any ideas about who might be mean enough to insult the dead body of a little lady."

"Right on," Lance said.

"Stay around through an eleven-to-seven shift at night. Don't make a big deal of it, just nose around without making it seem as if we're too concerned."

"When do I sleep?"

"When you need to. I'll deal your papers off to one of the other deputies. Take a couple of days or so. I just want to be sure this thing was one of a kind and there won't be any more tricks out there."

"I get the idea you're afraid there might be," Lance said.

"Well, a man mean enough to use a dead body like that, you can't tell. Maybe it was just a prank and someone will be laughing his ass off about it today. But there's just the chance that someone wants to see Bellamy closed bad enough to do something else. Old man like me don't want to see his hospital moved up into the Green Swamp."

Chapter Four

Burt Scoggins was feeling so bad that Dodo, who took his job seriously, was beginning to worry about his prisoner's health. Dodo offered water and aspirin and, as a last resort, offered to call his Aunt Tisha who had a reputation for miracle cures which made ole Doc Epstein jealous.

"No," Burt said, "it ain't aspirin I need."

It wasn't fair to have it there in plain sight, not when he was almost voluntarily serving a month of Saturday nights without so much as a drop to wet his cracked and drying throat. That evidence was more than his conscience and his good intentions could handle.

Burt had long experience at wheezling a drink. When it came to that, he could be as devious as any man. When he made up his mind and started working on Dodo, it was a classic mismatch. He kept telling Dodo how he felt so bad and how he liked to died once when he had to go two weeks without so much as a beer and how it was five weeks now and just about time for, judging by the way he felt, a Terminal Alcoholic Spasm. The way he said the words they rang in the empty jail. The very length of the words sounded like the crack of doom to Dodo, and Burt absolutely refused to let him call Aunt Tisha or even Jug.

"No, Dodo, we got to face it alone, you and me. Jest you and me, old friend. Nobody else. They cain't help us now. It's just you and me against them Terminal Alcoholic Spasms."

Burt's campaign started before breakfast. Dodo was so scared he didn't stop to figure out why he was in there fighting them spasms with Burt, and he worried when Burt didn't touch his breakfast of left over bluefish, fresh eggs, and grits. The battle raged on as the sun came up to light an achingly beautiful Saturday. From the window of his cell Burt could see the river and the small boats going out around the bend of the island to troll her blues. The beauty of the day was lost on him as he continued to work on Dodo until, just before noon, he judged that the psychological moment had arrived. He fell down onto the floor of the cell, legs stiff, only half pretending that he was having what very well might have become a Terminal Alcoholic Spasm. He gasped out to old Dodo that just a mouthful of the evidence would pull him through.

Dodo took about five minutes to decide that saving a man's life was more important than the evidence. Her climbed up on a broken chair and took down a half-gallon jar and poured about two ounces of it into a battered jailhouse mug and shoved it through the bars to Burt.

Burt had taken some fine drinks in his life, but never one to equal that white booze from the old, chipped mug. He'd been working on that thirst for five weeks, and the drink went down smooth as cream and tasting of heaven and pure alcohol. He felt it seep into his stomach lining, then warm and spread. He grinned and thanked Dodo for saving his life.

"You are a fine man," he told Dodo, "a jewel of a man, a gem of a man, one of the best. You deserve something for what you've done for me.

So, because of what you've done, I'm going to let you have a drink of the evidence."

Dodo overwhelmed by relief and praise said, "Why, thank you Burt. I always did believe in saving a man's life if I could."

Dodo wasn't much of a drinker. Usually he couldn't afford it. He had a shot now and then if someone offered, which wasn't often. He got down another coffee mug, a thick World War I Army mug of porcelain with chips on the rim, poured it half full, and sat down to enjoy it. He had a feeling that something was not quite right about Burt's offer, but his heart was still pounding from having seen Burt suffering a Terminal Alcoholic Spasm, and the corn was smooth, smooth.

"What we can do," Burt said, finishing off his drink and holding out his cup in two hands, as if afraid he might drop it, "is fill the jug back up with water. That way no one will know the difference. They'll still have the evidence while we, meanwhile, have a little taste or two."

"That makes sense," Dodo said, pouring.

Really good swamp-made white lightning is almost pure ethyl alcohol suspended in a bit of water. The alcohol, more mobile, more viscid, can be seen to move about inside the clean fruit jar, swirling in its aqueous solution with a hyponotic persistency. Good corn comes in at about one hundred and ninety proof. For an old man like Dodo two ounces of pure white liquor is instant party. Dodo felt the age melt from his bones, and he made no objection when Burt suggested another round.

Burt knew that he should lie down on his bunk now that that first terrible thirst was quenched and let Dodo put the evidence back on the shelf, but the devil wasn't going to allow that. The devil tilted the world and Burt felt the glow building and he couldn't just let such a glow die a natural death. He wouldn't let the old jailer fill the jar back up with water and put it on the shelf. He kept Dodo pouring until Dodo was completely soused. Dodo left the jar sitting next to the cell within Burt's reach and took a little practice nap. Burt lay back, mug resting on his chest, and tuned up his voice for verse one of a song about a drinking man who went to sea. It was not yet mid-afternoon. The one hundred and ninety proof alcohol, a full half gallon of it, would last a long, long time. There was no hurry.

P.J. Charlie knew about high proof alcohol. P.J. Charlie liberated medical alcohol from the lab at the hospital and mixed it with grape juice. A little bit went a long way and since P.J. was a good man in all other respects, a cracker-jack lab technician who was dependable and never late for work, even if a bit hung, no one ever said anything about the relatively minute amounts of alcohol liberated into Charlie's little half-pint flask. A half pint was party for six for a weekend.

P.J. was a tall, lanky brother with a head full of inky hair and a wild passion for girls of all descriptions. P.J. and Lance had grown up half a block apart and fought over and shared the same girls and the same jug of Purple Jesus. P.J. lived in a garage apartment next door to old John Hawkins, retired school principal. When Lance parked out front and went around back to the stairs and climbed them P.J. was sleeping off a Friday night on the town. He grumbled when Lance kept pounding on the door, but finally opened it. Lance went in and put on water for coffee and made a couple of pieces of toast and split them with P.J. Then P.J. was about half awake, wanting to know what was happening in the middle of the night.

"I wish I coulda seen their faces," Lance said.

"Who faces?"

"Del Pond and them other two nurses."

"I like to see more than that Del Pond's face," P.J. said, showing that his mind was now working along the usual lines.

"Musta been somethin'," Lance said.

"Man, I ain't gonna ask you what you talkin' 'bout."

"You ain't heard?"

"Heard what, man?"

"What you do last night?"

"This official business?" P.J. asked, drawing himself up.

"You know better than that."

"What you talkin'?"

"You ain't heard, I guess." With P.J., you couldn't be sure. It didn't sound like P.J.'s style. He liked his job and Lance was ninety-nine percent sure he wouldn't do anything to endanger it, but P.J. had been known to do some pretty weird things after a few ounces of his potent mixture. Lance told him about the incident at the hospital. P.J. was livid with indignation, and P.J. wasn't that much of an actor. The idea that anyone could do a thing like that in his hospital made P.J., as he put it, want to "kick a little ass."

"You 'vestigatin' this?" P.J. demanded.

"You can call it that."

"Well, let's get to it. I don't work on Saturday,

but I gotta go out and ship off some stuff. You wanta know anything 'bout that hospital you ask ole P.J. Charlie."

Lance followed P.J. Charlie's GTO out to the hospital and parked in the employees' parking lot. They went in the back doors beside the emergency room. The lab was halfway up the hall toward the receptionist's chair, which was unoccupied. As they walked up the hall Lance saw nurses and aides pushing the breakfast tables past the end of the hall down into the patient wing. P.J. pushed open the door to the lab and hit the light switch.

"You don't keep it locked?" Lance asked.

"No, man. Nurses might need to get in during the night."

"What you do in this lab?"

"Draw blood and run some simple tests. I can tell you got the VD."

"I wipe off all toilet seats," Lance said.

"Complicated stuff we farm out," P.J. Charlie said. "Like this stuff." He picked up a closed container of stainless steel. "This here's meat from the operating room. Female things, you dig? Gotta send 'em up to the state lab for biopsy, see they got cancer."

Lance was looking around. He'd been in the blood drawing room before. There were two schoolroom chairs with arms. You put your arm out and the female technician put a rubber band around your arm and stuck a needle in your vein and drew out some blood. There was a door between the drawing room and P.J.'s lab. In the lab, which was quite small, there were shelves of equipment and containers which meant nothing to Lance.

P.J. was moving around, getting out a smaller container for shipping the biopsy material, printing a label, talking now about girls. Lance moved to the door into the hall and there was a lot of activity going on. A wheel chair was being pushed up to the X-Ray lab across the hall and a smocked girl was smiling and talking to the old man in the chair. Down at emergency people were coming and going. Up the hall the receptionist was answering telephones, and now and then a nurse or an aide would pass the receptionist's desk. When he was in the hospital he'd been downstairs at first, in the intensive care room, and then, later, upstairs. He had also spent a couple of hours in the operating room upstairs somewhere, but he didn't remember that. He didn't like remembering any of it. It hurt. Not his shoulder. They kept that deadened with drugs. What hurt was remembering Glenda and the way she died at the hands of a madman. All for nothing. It hit him at odd times and the impact was like a hard tackle right in the gut. He was trying to get his mind on his business and off the past when P.J. Charlie said, "Son of a bitch."

He turned around. "It's gone," P.J. Charlie said. "My meat's gone."

The scream came then. It was muffled by distance. It seemed to seep from the walls, through the air ducts, down the hall. It was repeated, a sound of horror rather than pain, and those who were in the hallway halted and cocked their heads.

"What the hell?" P.J. Charlie said, looking up toward the ceiling. "Upstairs," he said, running down the hall toward the emergency room. The door to the rear stairs opened across from the emergency room entrance, a heavy fireproof metal door which banged behind them as Lance followed P.J. Charlie up the stairs. In the hallway of the second-floor ward a breakfast wagon sat outside one of the rooms near the stairwell. A chubby white nurse was running down from the nurses station at the far end. There was a sound of hysterical crying from the room nearest the breakfast cart. Lance skidded to a halt just as a black nurse came out of the room with a covered breakfast tray in her hands and fire in her eyes.

"P.J. Charlie, you no good," the nurse said.

"What's happening?" P.J. asked.

"As if you didn't know," the nurse said. She noticed Lance for the first time. "I'm glad you're here. I want you to arrest this no good, that's what's happening."

"You wanta slow down and tell me what's wrong?" Lance asked.

"This is what's wrong," the nurse said, lifting the metal cover.

The objects on the plate were obscenely wet, purplish, bloated.

"Like to give that poor woman a heart attack," the nurse said. "I never seen such in all my life."

"That's my meat," P.J. Charlie said. "Lance, that's my meat. Some filthy son of a bitch done stole it."

Ruben Epstein had started his morning rounds early in order to finish in time for an early start to his Saturday fishing. He, too, had heard the scream, but he had not been able to run up the stairs. He was puffing from having walked fast when he arrived and used his fiercest glare to quiet the gathering nurses. He shooed the nurses away

43

and took the tray. He motioned for Lance and P.J. to follow and went into the operating room.

"Now I want to know how this happened," he said sternly to P.J.

"Doc, I swear I don't know," P.J. said. "I left 'em in the lab, just like always when an operation is too late in the day to ship 'em out."

"What are you doing here, Lance?" Epstein asked. He'd done the repair job on Lance's shoulder.

"Jug told me to take a look around, do some talking about last night," Lance said. "Looks like I got something else to talk about now."

"I want this kept inside the hospital," Epstein said. "Do you both understand that?"

"Yes, sir," P.J. said.

"I'll ask Jug if I should file a report," Lance said.

"You do that," Epstein said.

"Just what are those things?" Lance asked.

Epstein had placed the covered tray on a table. He lifted the lid. "These are the internal organs of a forty-four-year-old woman." He pointed. "Ovaries, uterus, supportive and connective tissue. This small object is the vermiform appendix. They were removed yesterday afternoon just before four o'clock and delivered to the lab for shipment to the state hospital for biopsy."

"That means they were in the lab all night until someone removed them," Lance said. "Same joker who played around with the dead body?"

"It has the same macabre quality," Epstein said.

"Doc, you know I didn't do it," P.J. Charlie said, almost pleading. "Don't you know that?"

"I'm sure you wouldn't," Epstein said.

"Doc, you know of anyone real mad at you or this hospital?" Lance asked.

"There are always people mad at both me and the hospital," Epstein said. "We're a small hospital and we can't afford a large percentage of unpaid bills. We get rough in our collection techniques. We have to do it or close down. Then there's always someone who thinks he was overcharged or who thinks he wasn't treated properly. However, I still think when you find the sick mind which did these things you'll find it belongs to a hospital employee."

"You fired anyone lately? Anyone have some reason, right or wrong, to be particularly mad at the hospital?"

"You'd do best to talk with the administrator about that."

"I'll do that. But how about you? Any ideas of your own?"

"As far as I know we've got a good staff here."

"Doc, I think you'll see a lot of me in the next few days," Lance said. "Jug told me to hang around out here out of uniform."

"I appreciate that."

"Would the administrator be in now?"

"She usually works for a while on Saturday morning."

"How 'bout fingerprints on the tray?" P.J. Charlie asked.

"This ain't TV," Lance said. "We'll take 'em, all right, but how many people you seen handle that tray in the last few minutes?"

"Oh," P.J. Charlie said.

"P.J., you have these things in some sort of liquid?" Lance asked.

"Preservative solution," P.J. said.

"They look wet at first," Lance said, "but then you look closer and you see the outside of them is sorta dry and shiny. How long it take for them to dry out like that?"

"Least a hour or so."

"And the night shift went off at seven," Lance said. "Then lots of day people coming on, right?"

"Maybe you'd better call Jug," Epstein said.

"Later, Doc," Lance said. "Jug's not as young as he once was, and I suspect he's already back home taking a little after-breakfast nap. I'll do some preliminary footwork and then give him a call a little later."

"Whatever you think is best," Epstein said. "You wanta check with me if you come up with anything? I'll be here for at least another hour."

"Glad to, Doc," Lance said.

Epstein went out of the operating room, trailing ashes from his dangling cigarette. "You know," P.J. Charlie said, "when you're acting official you look a lot like Sidney Posterior."

"You and the horse you rode in on," Lance said. "You wanta bum around with me for a while?" P.J. nodded. "Show me the kitchen."

The kitchen was on the ground floor at the east end of the main portion of the building lying parallel to the street. It was presided over by Mrs. Evangelist Collins, a large, clean black woman with her hair covered totally by a white wraparound cap. She and her helper, a young black girl, were dishing up the last of the breakfasts when Lance followed P.J. into the large room which smelled of coffee and frying bacon.

"Nobody 'llowed in here," Mrs. Collins said.

If Lance had thought about it he would have remembered that Mrs. Collins was the hospital cook. He was thrown for a loss for a moment.

"Specially you, Lance Carver, or anyone wearing that uniform," Mrs. Collins said.

Evangelist Collins had special reason to dislike the Clarendon County Sheriff's Department. Her thirteen year old son Leafy had been one of the boys who died in the big shoot out in the Green Swamp, one of a group of young boys who had been organized and trained by the same man who had killed Glenda.

"I'm sorry, Mrs. Collins," Lance said, "but something has happened here in the hospital. I need to know a little about how you prepare and serve the food." He knew how she felt. All wounds don't leave scars.

"What you talkin'?" Mrs. Collins asked, holding a spatula in one hand, watching eggs frying with alternating, penetrating glares at Lance.

P.J. spoke before Lance could. "Stead of eggs and bacon one of the patients upstairs got a plate of leavings from the operating room."

"Lord God," Mrs. Collins said. "That the truth?"

"It's the truth," Lance said. "I'm trying to find out how it could have happened."

"Didn't happen here," Mrs. Collins said. "Not in my kitchen."

"Mrs. Collins, why don't you just tell me about this morning, how you came in and what you did and all?"

"Reckon it can wait," she said, turning to her grill. "We on a timetable here."

Lance stood aside and watched. The two women

had orders for each patient. The younger girl read them out and Mrs. Collins prepared them. Then the older girl placed the plates on a food cart, covered the plates with a metal cover, added coffee or milk and eating tools to the tray, put the name of the patient and the room number on a slip of paper in a clip holder. When the food cart was loaded, the girl pushed it to the door and Jimbo Rogers, the day shift orderly, pushed the cart down the hall to the nurses station. It was the last cart of the morning.

"I gets in 'round six," Mrs. Collins said. "I was jest a little late this morning, maybe five to ten minutes. Mary beat me here."

"Anything unusual about this morning?"

"Not I noticed," Mrs. Collins said. "Same as always. Weren't no meat from no operating room in my kitchen. I been off to school. This place is as 'ceptic as any operating room. Nothin' like that happen in my kitchen."

"Anyone come in during the morning?"

"Ain't nobody 'llowed in my kitchen."

"I don't want to be no bother, Miz Collins," Lance said, "but I might have to come back and talk to you."

"Well, 'fore you start shootin' kids and sick people, you let me know," Mrs. Collins said. "One Collins shot by the law is enough."

Lance wanted to tell her he had not fired his weapon up there in the Green Swamp. He wanted to tell her that he and Jug felt as bad about that as anyone. He wanted to tell her that an automatic weapon doesn't know how old the one using it is and that the soldiers and deputies who were killed in the swamp were just as dead as her Leafy, but he held back and didn't say anything.

They found Jimbo Rogers in the lower wing, carrying out a bedpan. Jimbo was nineteen, slim, almost effeminate in his manner. He wore hospital whites. His large eyes were framed by metal wraparound glasses. He emptied the bedpan in the toilet and came out of the room.

"I need to talk to you, Jimbo," Lance said.

"Figured you would," Jimbo said. He led the way out the back door and lit a cigarette. There was a small stoop at the rear of the west wing. "I didn't do it, Lance."

"We're just trying to find out who did. How many food carts went up to the second floor?"

"Just the one. They have three empty rooms up there at the moment."

"Just tell me what you did this morning," Lance said.

"I come on at seven, like always. Night shift goes off. I work the first floor. Went down to help the old man in room seven pee. Had a cup of coffee at the nurse's station. Rolled a lady down to X-Ray in a wheel chair. Nothing unusual."

"O.K., you didn't see anyone shouldn't be in the hospital?"

"Well, you know we don't go too close by visiting hours here, small hospital and friendly. Folks goes to work early they sometimes stop by and see family on the way. Maybe a couple of visitors, I didn't particularly notice. No one out of the ordinary."

"When did they start serving breakfast?"

"At eight. Miz Collins has the first cart loaded right on the button. It goes upstairs."

"The first cart?"

"Right."

"And how does it get up there?"

Jimbo flipped his cigarette away. "Best I show you." He led the way down the hall, around the corner, past the nurse's station, and into the main corridor leading to the emergency room. The elevator was halfway down the hall. "I rolled the cart into the elevator and pushed the button for two and then got out."

"So the cart goes up by itself in the elevator?"

"It did this morning. No one going up."

"Jimbo you got any idea how the switch could have been made and where?"

"I don't know. I went on back to the kitchen for another cart."

"How do the nurses upstairs know the cart is coming up?"

"Like I say, Miz Collins, she has it ready on the dot of eight. They know it's gonna be there couple of minutes after."

"This detective business is a drag, man," P.J. Charlie said as they rode up on the elevator. "I think I cut out and head beachwise."

"Yeah," Lance said, "no use you hanging 'round."

P.J. went back down on the elevator. Lance stepped out into the hall. The black nurse was seated at the nurses station at the T of the hall. "You arrest that no good P.J. Charlie?" she demanded.

Lance looked at the name plate on the starched white uniform. "Mrs. Cates, is it?"

"That's right."

"You're not from Earlysburg."

"Live out in the country this side of Swansey."

"I don't think P.J. Charlie did it," Lance said. "Since he was with me."

"Maybe you helped," Mrs. Cates said.

"You're a real clown, aren't you?"

"Not clown enough to scare a poor woman half to death."

"How many on the second floor daytime?"

"Two RN's, one aide and the orderly."

"Who took the food cart off the elevator?"

"I took it off myself. Had to push the button get the elevator back up."

"The elevator came up and then went back down with the food cart still in it?" Lance asked.

"Does that sometimes, someone wanta come up. Sometimes we be busy when it comes up and someone wanta ride up they push the button and the elevator goes back down and then they come up."

"Who came up this morning?"

"Not a soul."

"So you were busy—"

"Woman in two-oh-two wanting a pain pill. She couldn't have one because she'd just been given one a couple of hours before."

"Where were the others?" Lance asked.

"Morning medication, other RN checking on an IV in that poor woman operated on yesterday, the aide handing out pills, the orderly taking care of a bedpan call."

"How about the patients?"

"We low right now. Got just eleven up here, all clean patients on the second floor."

"Clean?"

"Nothing catching. This is the ward where we keep surgery patients and heart and accident patients. Flu and like that down below."

"How many of the patients are able to get up and walk around?"

"Let's see. Got three hearts on oxygen. They could get up, I guess, but they might not make it to the door. One heart recuperating. He goes to the bathroom, but he's weak. Then there's the hysterectomy and the gall bladder, they ain't going nowhere yet."

"Just the ones can walk," Lance said.

"One man in traction, the three accidents, they all banged up, one of 'em move a little but he hurt when he does. Miz Watson with the broken hip. H-mm. We got two patients can move around freely, the lady who was served the meat and a six-year-old-girl had her tonsils out."

"I guess that takes care of that," Lance said. "And you didn't see anyone in the halls shouldn't have been there?"

"It could have been done up here," Mrs. Cates said, "but I don't know. I'd guess downstairs. More people moving around down there."

P.J. Charlie was coming out of the lab when Lance rode the elevator down. He had a package in his hands. "The meat goes off," he said, lifting the package.

"P.J., that plate the meat was on, it have anything on it like egg or bacon grease?"

"Clean," P.J. said. "Musta switched the whole plate or the whole thing, cover and all."

"Then somewhere around here there's got to be a breakfast plate," Lance said.

"You right," P.J. said. He looked up and down the hall. "Closest door is X-Ray."

The X-ray technician was having a cup of coffee, no customers at the moment. Lance told her what he was looking for and she said, "No place to hide it in here." She was a white girl in her late twenties, Lance guessed, not overly attractive.

"Mind if we look around anyhow?"

"Be my guest."

"What's in the closet here?"

"Photographic paper. It stays locked." As she spoke Lance was reaching for the doorknob. The door opened. "I'll be damned," the girl said. Lance saw the covered plate on a shelf atop a stack of brown envelopes. He put his hands all the way under it and lifted it out to place it on the X-ray table, then used two pens to lift the cover without touching it. Under the cover were scrambled eggs, bacon and toast.

"You being careful so you can get fingerprints?" P.J. asked, eyes wide.

"Won't hurt to try," Lance said. He turned to the X-ray technician. "Door is locked, huh?"

"Beats me," she said. "I locked it when I left here last night."

"Who else got a key?"

"The other tech. She's off today. I don't know of anybody else." She had put her coffee aside and there was a concerned look on her face. "Look, I don't like this. I don't like this a bit."

"I don't think the lady upstairs liked it either," Lance said.

"I mean, someone comes messing around in my lab and tries to put the blame on me—"

"No one is putting any blame anywhere yet," Lance said.

"I was busy right from the time I came in at seven until just a few minutes ago."

"What happened then?"

53

"I mean I had people, patients, in and out of here taking X-rays until almost eight o'clock."

"And what then?"

"I went down to the nurses station for a cup of coffee."

"Aha," P.J. Charlie said.

"I thought you were heading beachwise," Lance said.

"I gonna cut out in a minute, dah," P.J. Charlie said in a deep, comic voice. "First I's gonna straighten you out, law boy." He turned to the X-ray tech. "May I borrow your key, madam?" She handed over the key and P.J. Charlie locked the closet door. He handed the key back and then leaned against the door, pushing it tightly inward, twisting the doorknob and then giving a quick jerk. The door opened. "Evelyn, the other tech, she's always losing her key. Had me try to open the door one day and I discovered that the lock don't make good contact and a little pull is all it needs."

"Just great," Lance said. "That's just great. I wonder how many other people know that little trick."

"Wouldn't take much intelligence to look at it and see it wasn't making good contact," P.J. Charlie said.

"O.K., P.J.," Lance said. "Go make your shipment."

P.J. grinned and pointed his finger at the X-ray tech. "If you got any ideas 'bout leavin' town, forget 'em."

"Get out of here, Charlie," Lance said.

The business offices were lighted. There were three women in the open section of the office next to the waiting room and the door to the administrator's office was open. Lance stuck his head in.

"Come in," Helen Royce said. She was a tall, straight, cool, blond woman. Lance estimated her to be on the wrong side of forty-five. She was dressed neatly in a suit of light gray. Her desk reflected her neatness of appearance. Her voice was strong, almost harsh. She had the no nonsense look of the professional, unmarried career woman.

Lance took off his hat and sat down in front of the desk. "I guess you've heard."

"Damned right I have, and I want something done about it," she said. "It's disgraceful, unforgivable. And with the hospital being threatened from all sides."

"How's that?" Lance asked.

"You must know that there is a concerted political effort to close Bellamy," Miss Royce said.

"I've heard a little bit," Lance said. "Maybe you can brief me on the situation."

"You know of course, that the voters passed a bond referendum to finance the building of a new hospital."

Lance nodded.

"Location of a new building was not a part of the referendum. However, since the majority of support for Bellamy comes from the eastern end of the county, it seems logical not to move the hospital too far away from Earlysburg and the beach area. The political organization centered in Swansey has different ideas, and they're doing all they can to move any new hospital to what they call a central location. Meaning, as they see it, out on Highway 17 near Swansey. They have a majority of the County Board of Commissioners on their side.

And to complicate matters, Bellamy is officially a county hospital, although no county funds have been contributed to the hospital in the past ten years. Actually, it's more an Earlysburg hospital than a county hospital. Because of the size of the county, those who live in the northern areas go into Wilmington for medical treatment, the people in the western areas go to Columbus Memorial and those in the south into the Grand Strand area. Actually, Bellamy pulls most of its patients from the eastern end of the county and a large portion of its operating costs is met by Earlysburg tax money."

"Do you think someone out in the county might be willing to risk going to jail to discredit Bellamy?" Lance asked.

"Who knows what people will do?" Miss Royce asked. "One of the members of the Board of Commissioners is trying to sell the county a plot of land for hospital location." She smiled thinly. "At a considerable advance over usual prices for undeveloped slash pine land, I might add."

"Is that common knowledge or rumor?" Lance said.

"You should read the newspapers," she said.

"The local weekly doesn't have any comic pages," Lance said.

She gave him a cold look. "At the moment, there is a movement underway to move toward a two hospital concept. A new hospital will be built, eventually, and since the western area of the county crries more votes, it will probably be built at some distance from Earlysburg. There will be problems. It's extremely difficult to attract doctors to a town as small as Earlysburg. With big money available to doctors in larger areas, it takes a special breed of man to want to live in a small coastal town. If you'll think about it, the doctors we have here have one thing in common."

"They're all fishermen," Lance said. "Like Doc Epstein."

"Or they simply enjoy living near the ocean. They're willing to settle for less money to live in a quiet town where they can allow their children some freedom of movement. There is not a single one of them who is willing to move inland should the new hospital be built in the Swansey area. The county will end up with a white elephant without staff, without nurses, without doctors. Or, at best, the county will have to subsidize doctors to lure them to the Swansey area and that would be quite incongruous, fishermen making six thousand a year paying taxes to provide free office space for doctors with a potential of thirty thousand and more per year."

"Deputies making not much more than six thousand wouldn't like that, either," Lance grinned.

"With medical costs the way they are," Miss Royce said, "it's a very unusual hospital which is self-supporting, and it's almost impossible for a small hospital like Bellamy to meet its own expenses. Hospitals like Bellamy exist only with the help of government and private institution grants. In addition to Earlysburg tax money, Bellamy receives money from the state and federal governments and from the Duke Endowment Fund. We are subject to approval by state agencies and federal agencies. We must maintain certain standards. State agencies also have a say in whether or not there will be one or two hospitals in Clarendon County. A ruling has already been handed down. The state says that Clarendon cannot support two hospitals. If there were two hospitals, one, perhaps, might starve because there just isn't enough money to go around. In order to qualify for grants in aid, a new hospital would have to compete with Bellamy, and as long as we can meet minimum standards, it would be difficult for the state to withdraw our accreditation. Therefore, it is vital to those who support a new, single hospital to see Bellamy closed."

"So politics and money rear their heads," Lance said.

"Don't they always?" she asked.

"Dr. Epstein thinks it's someone who works here," Lance said.

"That seems logical. I suppose an outsider could learn enough about our operation from observation while visiting a patient, but it seems unlikely, doesn't it?"

"He'd have to be one swift dude," Lance said. "Have to know the procedure for shipping off, uh, things from the operating room. Have to know about a trick lock in X-ray—"

"What's that?"

"I found the breakfast tray which had been switched in the X-ray room closet. If you jerk the door just right the lock opens."

"Rather esoteric knowledge," Miss Royce said.

"I think a good place to start would be a list of all hospital employees arranged by shifts," Lance said. "I want particularly to know who was officially on duty last night on the eleven-to-seven shift."

"I'll have one of the girls type it up for you."

"Meantime, I want to run a fingerprint check on

the breakfast trays. I probably won't be around during the afternoon and early evening, but I'll spend some time here with the eleven-to-seven people."

"If there's anything at all I can do to help, you'll find my home telephone number on the list at the switchboard."

Chief Deputy Dennis Watts was in the office when Lance arrived with the two breakfast trays, the one which had been hidden in the X-ray room closet and the other which had held the organs from the operating room. Watts was a detail man. He did most of the fingerprint work for the department, and he was good at it. Lance provided him with prints of the people who had legitimate reason to handle any of the objects on the trays. Evangelist Collins had protested until he explained to her the importance of her putting her fingers into ink and pressing them onto the card. The others let him take their prints willingly.

Lance explained the food handling procedure to Watts, and told him to expect to find the prints of the cook and her helper and possibly the prints of the day orderly on the tray from the closet. On the other tray, which had hidden the grisly secrets of a woman's interior, there would be prints from Mrs. Cates, the upstairs nurse who had served the tray, and from Dr. Epstein, in addition to the others. Finding the orderly's prints on the food tray would not necessarily be incriminating.

The chief deputy had already checked the rubber hose which had held Marian Powers to the receptionist's chair with negative results. The material was not conducive to holding prints. He would get on the trays and their contents immediately.

Lance's next stop was at the public library. He spent two hours reading through back issues of the local weekly newspaper. He had not realized that the hospital fight had become so bitter. There'd always been rivalry between Swansey and Earlysburg, but the hospital issue was creating more hot feelings than anything had in recent years.

A central hospital location was being pushed for by a group of Swansey businessmen and attorneys and by a majority of the County Board of Commissioners. In opposition, the town government of Earlysburg, claiming that it was their tax money which met the hospital's deficits, were claiming Bellamy as a city hospital, and the Board of Commissioners were near agreement, evidently thinking that making the hospital solely an Earlysburg hospital would strengthen their position to make it possible to close Bellamy completely upon completion of the new hospital.

Lance made notes and carried them in his pocket when he drove to Fortier Beach to find Jug weeding his garden. Jug was ready for a break. They sat in lawn chairs under the trees, swatting the occasional mosquito. Jug was shocked by the latest incident at the hospital.

"These things come in threes, boy," he said. "You'll want to keep your eyes open."

"I'll do that, Sheriff Honk," Lance said grinning.

"How many times I gotta tell you, to me you are a boy, a lad. Hell, you're just twenty-four," Jug said.

"Twenty-five in ten days," Lance said.

"And I'm sixty-four going on sixty-five in a couple of months and that's the way I talk, boy."

"Right on, Sheriff Honk."

"Were I prejudiced, I'd have your black ass out in the county 'stead of on the best beat in the department," Jug said.

"Then you'd have to find another black to be your token nigger in the office," Lance said. "And someone who knows everyone in the black community."

Jug spat tobacco juice and looked at Lance for a long moment. "You don't really feel that way."

Lance grinned. "We blacks are supposed to rebel now and then."

"You've done good work, boy. Getting shot and all I wasn't sure you'd want to go on with it. But you did and that makes you a man in my eyes, but damnit, I knew you and your family when you was runnin' around in diapers." Jug sighed. "Well, I've learned how to say black instead of Negra. Give me credit for trying."

"You'll make it yet, Jug," Lance said, laughing.

"Well, now that we've got the race problem solved again—"

"It's still a good bet that someone in the hospital did it," Lance said. "But I've been doing some reading about the whole situation. There's a possibility I might need to talk with some of the big wheels in the move-the-hospital movement and I wonder if that would be a good idea."

"Why not?"

"Well, big lawyers and big politicians and all."

"You need any help you let me know."

"You think someone might be serious enough about moving the hospital to do those things or hire them done? I was talking with Miss Royce and she says the hospital has to meet minimum standards or the state closes them down and takes away grant money."

"Anything is possible," Jug said. "But I'd bet on some employee mad at something."

"I meant to ask Miss Royce about that," Lance said. "Use the telephone?" He went inside. Jug's wife, Bessie, was working up a blueberry cobler. She asked Lance to stay for lunch and Lance said he had to get on back to town.

Helen Royce was still in her office. She told Lance that there'd been little change in the staff in the past few months. A nurse's aide had quit to take another job and a registered nurse had resigned to work in a larger hospital out of state. The administrator could think of no one who might have a grudge against the hospital.

"We run a tight shop," she said, "but I think everyone likes to know what's expected of him, and that if he goofs he's going to be called onto the carpet for it."

"Anyone goof lately?" Lance asked.

"Not really. I had a talk with the switchboard girl about leaving the telephones disconnected when she leaves for the night. Unless the telephones upstairs are patched through there is no service on the second floor, but that was a minor thing."

Lance reported the negative information to Jug and sat in the shade for a few minutes while Jug bragged about the yield of his Better Boy tomatoes. On the way to town he stopped off at the hospital and picked up the lists of hospital employees. He had a barbecue plate at The Spot and then went home to put on the new Nancy Wilson record he'd discovered in a bargain bin on his last trip to Wilmington. He fell asleep before the record was finished. He'd always been able to sleep almost any time, but since his wound he found himself needing more sleep. When he was asleep he dreamed occasionally, but at least he didn't have to think about how Glenda had looked after Jack Boydston used the knife on her, opening up her stomach cavity.

The telephone woke him just after five o'clock. Dennis Watts had found many fingerprints on the tray, the cover and the other items on the tray, the prints of Mrs. Collins, the cook, and her helper.

P.J. Charlie woke him again before his alarm went off at ten o'clock. P.J. had two little honey bears with him and wanted Lance to go for a ride. The girls followed P.J. Charlie into the living room, giggling, the taller one looking at Lance with an unmistakable challenge. Lance had one drink from P.J. Charlie's purple jug and sent them off to party alone. He pulled P.J. Charlie back inside after the girls had gone out the door.

"Man, when I'm ready for that I don't need no pimp," he said. P.J. Charlie had, it seemed, decided that it had been long enough. He was always trying to fix Lance up with a fox.

"O.K., man," P.J. Charlie said, "but it ain't natural."

Lance changed into slacks and shirt after taking a quick shower, ate a bowl of cerial and two pieces of toast and was getting ready to drive out to the hospital when the telephone rang again.

"Get your ass out to the hospital," the night man in the office said.

"I was just on my way," Lance said. "What's up?"

"Something about blood in the kitchen."

"You call Jug?"

"Jug's on his way to town. Must have his radio turned off because I can't get him. I called him just a few minutes ago on another matter."

"Well, keep trying to get him," Lance said, "and I'm on my way now."

He used the lights and touched the siren once when his way was blocked by two cars driving abreast on the main street. It was five minutes to eleven when he pulled into the nurses' parking lot and ran into the hospital through the front door. He turned right and there were several people, nurses, aides, an orderly and a tall, handsome man, standing in and around the kitchen doors.

Mrs. Collins' neat kitchen was a gory mess. The rich, ripe smell of blood was in the air. Blood had been poured over the work tables, the range, and the racks of dishes. Blood had been slung onto the walls. It pooled on the otherwise spotless floor. Food supplies, flour, salt, sugar, and rice had been poured atop the counters and mixed with blood.

The oncoming eleven-to-seven shift was mixed in with the offgoing three-to-eleven shift. There were almost a dozen people in the halls. Lance knew some of them. He knew Mrs. Lowery and Betty Mae Scoggins. He knew Delphi Pond. She'd been on the second floor while he was hospitalized.

He got the attention of everyone and asked if anyone had seen anything or anybody. Betty Mae Scoggins had discovered the mess. Coming on shift a few minutes early, she'd gone into the kitchen to get fresh cream for the night's coffee.

"I'm gonna quit running errands around this place," she said, looking first at Lance and then at Mrs. Lowery and Delphi. "First I walk up and find a dead body and then this."

Chapter Five

Burt Scoggins was a happy drunk. When he was carrying a load he felt so good he asked only the opportunity to share his high spirits with other people. That was his downfall. If he had been the kind of drinking man who hits the bottle in his own home or puts away the suds with the boys down at the Fore and Aft Bar and Grill, he would never have been hauled up before the judge and he wouldn't have been serving a month in the jug a weekend at a time. When Burt got loaded he had to let the world know how good he felt. At such times he would take himself to a public place and start to entertain. His one song was about a sea-going man, skipper of the schooner called the *Peter Pan*, who, throughout his long and honorable career, steadfastly insisted on saving the alcohol.

Burt had been trying to teach Dodo the verses to the song about ole Bucker-Mouth McGinty, but Dodo was a failure. He knew nothing about close harmony and, besides, he was always falling asleep, and then Burt would have to drink and sing alone. Dodo was too soused even to be a good audience. Burt yelled Dodo into wakefulness, more or less, and told Dodo that he would like to step out for a breath of air. Dodo waved a limp hand. Burt kept at him until Dodo staggered over to the desk and got the key to the cell.

Burt passed the judge coming out of the drugstore on the main corner. Burt nodded and spoke. The judge was so used to seeing Burt downtown on a Saturday night, slightly or more than slightly drunk, that he merely nodded in return, thinking that he would probably be seeing Burt in court come Monday morning.

Burt made his way to the theater. The show was still going on, but there were a few teenagers hanging around outside. A couple of the older boys even knew some of the choruses from previous Burt Scoggins concerts. Burt sang twenty-five verses of "Old Bucket-Mouth McGinty" before the show let out, and two of the little old ladies of the town came out to stare at him with open disapproval.

Once when Burt was in the Air Force he had sung thirty verses of "Old Bucket-Mouth McGinty" in a bar in Mobile, including three or four he made up himself. That night would always stand out in his memory, but the night in front of the theater with the moon coming up over the river, full and beautiful, and the night air sweet as wine was almost as fine. He was fulfilled. He'd also been away from the jug for over an hour and a half. He walked back to the jail feeling better than he'd felt in a long time. He was thinking, now his mission to entertain was accomplished, of his duty.

In Burt's absence, Dodo, being able to drink as much as he wanted to without anyone looking at him as if he were a moocher, was working on the evidence. He tried to sing a little, but he'd never been able to carry a tune, so he sat on the floor with his back against the desk and went to sleep.

When Burt came in the first thing he did was

have a taste, then he started talking to Dodo about how bright the stars were and how the river was just wiggling a little under a mild southeast wind and how pretty soon it would be autumn and the speckled trout would start to hit a white grub in the creeks over behind the island. It was a long time before Burt noticed that Dodo wasn't making any contribution to the conversation. Burt had another little taste to help him think it over. Dodo didn't answer. Dodo didn't move. Burt put his hand on Dodo's shoulder and the old man slid limply to the floor.

Burt felt a surge of overwhelming sadness. He had another taste to help him overcome the urge to shed tears, and then he decided he'd better call Jug. It wasn't right just to leave poor old Dodo just lying there. He called Jug and told him that there was something terribly wrong with poor old Dodo. He hung up and had another one from the now pretty well fractured half-gallon jar. All the joy was gone out of the night because poor old Dodo was dead, lying there on the floor with his poor white old hair all wet with sweat.

Just before Jug's car came around the corner up by the church, moving fast but not recklessly fast, Dodo moved and groaned and mumbled, "Ole Bucket-Mouth McGinty wash quite a drinkin' man." He wasn't carrying the tune. Burt's heart leaped up and the world, once again, was a joy, except that he and old Dodo were both going to be in a heap of trouble. Jug's car was stopping outside the chainlink fence. Burt had to have some time to repair the damage to the evidence. He ran into the yard and locked the padlock on the gate just as Jug was getting out of the car.

"Burt, dern you," Jug yelled, as Burt ran back inside the jail and slammed the door. He rattled the gate, but his key to the padlock was at home atop a marbletop table in the bedroom. And there was the prisoner running loose after calling on the telephone to say that something was wrong with the jailer.

Jug was too old to climb the fence and his yelling brought no response from inside the jail. He got in his car and took off, getting a wheel in the gravel. He made it to the beach and back in twenty minutes, using the lights, and when he got inside the fence he could see Burt out of the cell, sitting on the floor beside old Dodo trying to force the old man to drink something out of a cup. Burt, he could see, was drunk as a lord. Jug yelled and pounded on the door, but he was very securely locked out of his own jail. He wasn't thinking of it being an election year. He was just mad. He yelled and kicked on the door until he roused Miss Claudette Gillette, the town's amateur historian and a self-appointed policer of the public morals. Miss Claudette called her nephew, who was, as it happened, the only Republican on the supposedly nonpartisan Town Board of Aldermen. Miss Claudette reported that Jug Watson was blind out of his mind and yelling obscenities down at the jail.

Inside, Burt was still determined, with drunken logic, to sober up Dodo before he let Jug in. Ronnie Gillette, the Republican alderman, gathered up a few sympathizers and went down to the jail. When he saw the situation, Gillette snickered and sent a boy to call out the Volunteer Fire Department. The wail of the fire siren brought the usual crowd of engine chasers and Jug had himself an audience.

He took off his hat and wiped his brow. It was time for serious action. It was, after all, an election year and here he was, sheriff almost for life or for as long as he wanted it, locked out of his own jail by a prisoner who had, with the help of the jailer, ruined half the evidence in a moonshine case.

"Stand back," Jug shouted, as the firemen and the alderman advanced. He jerked out his pistol which hadn't been fired in almost six months, not since he killed a copperhead snake out in the back yard. The gun roared with brutal authority and the old doorlock shattered.

"You are under arrest," Jug said to Burt, who by that time had Dodo sitting up against the desk again.

"Why, I know that, Jug," Burt said.

"Just get back in the cell, Burt," Jug said, sighing, as his audience crowded into the jail. Burt walked most unsteadily into the cell, humming. He closed the door behind him, locked it, and put the key in his pocket.

"All right, you folks," Jug said, "the show's over. You can go on home now." He began shoving people out of the jail, but Alderman Gillette stayed.

"You might need some help with this vicious criminal, Jug," Gillette said, playing it for laughs. A young lawyer, a member of the Volunteer Fire Department and on the opposite side of the political fence, laughed.

"Sheriff," the young lawyer said, "who's going to pay for the damage of county property?" He fingered the splintered wood around the doorlock.

Jug went up to the bars of the cell and whispered, "Burt, you want to give me the key to the cell?"

Burt pretended not to hear. He launched into a fresh rendition of his one song. Jug sighed wearily and pulled the chair out from the desk and sat down, putting his feet up. His thought was to wait it out. They'd get tired of the fun after a while and go home and then he'd get the key from Burt and it would all be just a little joke on him.

But after an hour which included to Burt's delight, three new and spontaneous verses of "Old Bucket-Mouth McGinty," Jug began to get suspicious. With the fuel removed from the fire, Burt should have been cooling off.

"It would almost seem," Alderman Gillette said, "that the prisoner has something alcoholic in his cell."

There wasn't anything in Burt's cell except a few king-sized coke bottles of water, but Jug walked to the shelf and took down the remaining jar of evidence and sniffed it. He tasted it and instead of it being pure alcohol it was almost all water. One of the things that Burt had done while Jug was locked out was to pour the contents of the second jug of evidence into the king-sized coke bottles.

"It's going to be a long night," Jug said as Burt laughed happily and launched into another inspired new verse.

Chapter Six

Dennis Watts, in spite of what some may have thought, did not want to be sheriff. The chief deputy had two main passions and they were contradictory. In effect, the achievement of one of his desires cancelled out the other, for he wanted, number one, to have time to become the best yellow-fin trout fisherman in the world and, two, to work in and perhaps be in charge of a modern crime laboratory. In order to practice the art of catching yellow-fin trout, he needed to live in Clarendon County and venture out of Cape Fear in his McKee Craft as often as possible to see if the yellow-fins had moved on to one of the three or four sunken wrecks which were his favorite fishing spots. If he lived in Clarendon County, he'd have to be very long-lived to ever see the county be large enough and rich enough for the Sheriff's Department to have the sort of lab he'd want.

Once married and now divorced, Dennis was forty-six, medium short but trim, and had a head full of wavy black hair. He did not bother to tint the gray which was beginning to sprinkle it. He wore glasses when reading or doing close work, his uniform was always immaculate, and he had a ready laugh which made people like him at first and then withdraw slightly upon further exposure to his finicky personality. Dennis demanded perfection of himself and of others. Lasting relationships cannot be based on such demands.

Dennis played the clarinet well enough to sit in now and then with the band which worked weekends at the Fidler's Basin Restaurant on the beach. He liked mathematical puzzles and he did much of the maintenance on his aging Bonanza which was parked under the shed at the Clarendon County Airport out by the Waterway bridge. He owned just over two hundred acres of Clarendon, rented the cleared areas of his land to farmers, intended never to marry again, and never touched the cash which had come to him from his father along with the Clarendon land, not after the one and only withdrawal from capital to pay for the Bonanza. He helped pay expenses on the aircraft by renting it to carefully screened local flyers and by, every now and then, flying a body for Bridge Truval, the local undertaker and county coroner. The Bonanza's cabin was not large enough to accomodate a coffin, so when a body was flown it was bagged and placed on a plywood coffin-shaped board which Dennis had cut himself, which was placed on the right side of the cabin head to the rear, spanning back and front seats, putting the feet up next to Dennis. Body flying paid well.

Flying Marian Powers' body to the State Forensic Medicine Lab on Saturday morning paid only a little because Dennis gave the county a low rate. He needed to fly into Raleigh to get an estimate on some required engine work, so he combined his business with department business.

As usual, all the detail work had been left to him. He didn't mind. He was the one who had gone through the dead woman's personal effects and delivered them early that morning to Sage Jeffrie, the attorney who handled all of Miss Marian's affairs. Dennis sent a deputy to see that Miss Marian's town home on the river was locked and that there were also padlocks on the beach cottage. Dennis was known for his efficiency, and the things that he accomplished were taken for granted by Jug and other members of the department.

During his brief talk with Sage Jeffrie he had been told about Miss Marian's will and, aside from Sage, he was the only man in Clarendon who knew how much money Miss Marian had left to Bellamy Memorial Hospital. He would not pass the world along. People talked to Dennis because they knew he would respect the confidence. He could, however, have told Ruben Epstein that his estimate of a million of dollars was far short. Miss Marian's liquid assets and her stocks and bonds added almost to the estimated million, and on top of that Bellamy Memorial Hospital, providing that it remain within the immediate area of Earlysburg, would own the finest large tract of development land in the county. The future worth of that land could make Bellamy a fairly rich institution.

Dennis was pleasantly surprised by Jug's having ordered an autopsy. It would not have surprised him if Miss Marian had been slipped quietly into the ground or sent off for the medical students at Duke. Sometimes Jug, having been sheriff for so long, tended to use his own judgement to protect the county or even to protect old and honored citizens of the county. He never flouted the law seriously, just took a shortcut now and then, but then shortcuts were taken in the presence of power and prestige all over the world. The law for a prominent citizen was different from the law for a drifter or a common working man.

Dennis was aware of the curious incidents at Bellamy Hospital. He did not like the smell of it. Millions of dollars, the existence of the hospital at stake, political pressure from out in the county, all these things plus a movable corpse and grisly pranks aroused Dennis' interest. Dr. Epstein did not stand to gain personally from Miss Marian's death, not in the form of a direct deposit to his bank account, but it was well known that since coming to practice in Earlysburg twenty years ago Epstein had taken a most passionate interest in the small, failing hospital and had, almost on his own back, kept it going. Widowed and childless, the hospital was Epstein's wife and child.

Dennis was a member of several flying clubs around the state and as a result he had a wide range of friends. One of his friends flew an Apache and was second in command at the forensic lab. By coincidence, Dennis' friend was working that weekend and had some time on his hands. When Dennis delivered the body in a state-owned hearse, only minutes elapsed before Miss Marian went under the knife. Dennis watched the first stages with an avid curiosity. He admired the skill of the team. He liked the ring of the medical jargon, the aura of competence, and the sense of seriousness with which his friend went about the job of disassembling Miss Marian for the sake of total knowledge of the cause of her death.

Since the presence of the drug epinephrine was known in advance the autopsy team looked for hyperemia and found it. Dennis' friend explained that hyperemia was simply a condition of engorgement of organs with blood as the result of the fatal dilation of blood vessels, a definite reaction to epinephrine.

The work was not completed, but Dennis' friend motioned him outside into the hall and lit a cigarette.

"She got a real slug of it," the MD said. "How'd such a stupid thing happen?"

"She was being given point-three cc's per hour subcutaneously," Dennis said.

"No way," the MD said. "She got one hellofa lot more than that. We can't tell without some measurements, but I'll bet you a steak dinner on a minimum dose of ten cc's and maybe as much as sixty."

"No bet," Dennis said. "That would change the entire picture."

"I'll bet. Local doctor?"

"Yes," Dennis said.

"Too bad. Probably find that there was a slipup in the orders, bad writing, poor attention on the part of a nurse. But for the life of me I don't see how anyone could give such an overdose. That stuff is usually packaged in ampules with just enough for a standard dose."

"In volume, how much would ten cc's of the drug be?" Dennis asked.

"Depends on the solution. At a thousand to one, it would be a lot of liquid. But it's also used as an inhalant, and then it's about a ten percent mixture. The quantity of fluid needed to build up about ten mg of the drug, a fatal dose, would be lessened greatly."

"Enough so to make it possible to inject a fatal dose with one syringe?" Dennis asked.

"Yes, but then it would have had to be deliberate, wouldn't it?"

Dennis nodded. "You mean an empty syringe would have had to be filled with the solution and that the person filling it would know what he was doing. He would know that he was giving an overdose, because the usual dose is in a little ampule, right?"

"Right. Sounds to me, if it proves out there's as much of it in her as I think, that you've got yourself a homicide, Dennis my boy."

Dennis was almost sorry Jug had ordered the autopsy. It was going to be mean and nasty trying to close the file on this one.

"We need this," he said, "like we need a kick in the ass."

"Probably the worst that can happen is disgrace for a doctor or a nurse and a malpractice suit," his friend said.

But Dennis was thinking of politics and the hospital, the passions it aroused and an estate worth millions.

Chapter Seven

It was the most glorious drunk Burt had ever had. He had an audience. His friend Jug sat there listening as he made up verses and there was the alderman and the nice young lawyer and from time to time others would stop in. They came all the way from Swansey to speak to Jug with a knowing little smile, and to listen to Burt sing about the final wreck of the ill-fated schooner the *Peter Pan*. Burt was in his best voice and his mind was working miracles with invention and rhyme. It was a glorious night. He wanted it to go on forever.

It went on forever as far as Jug was concerned. Early on, he considered taking the citadel of Burt's happiness by brute force, but the jail was a well constructed building and the bars were old fashioned steel, hard as steel used to be, and county property not to be lightly destroyed. Moreover, if Jug did what he felt like doing, blast the cell with a dozen sticks of dynamite, then it might do some little damage to Burt and the bystanders.

Jug decided to play it lightly. He would show his humane consideration for a poor helpless alcoholic. He laughed and joked with the young lawyers who came all the way from Swansey to chuckle at his embarrassment until his face hurt with the effort.

When the reporter from the local weekly came

with his camera and notebook Jug pulled him aside. "Popeye," he said, "I can't tell you not to print this, but what I can tell you is that you've had a lot of tips from this department in the past."

"Ah, Jug," the reporter said, "this would be good for a feature on the AP wire. I don't get a shot at many of these."

"Go right ahead," Jug said. "One last good story from this department might make up for the long drought ahead."

Popeye wanted to cry a little, but he joined the group in the jail instead and watched them come and go. Then the Wilmington TV crew arrived in the dead of night, one and a half hours past midnight. Jug knew he was treed. He gave an interview and the girl TV reporter played it for laughs. Then the camera went inside with a bright light. Burt, in hog heaven, stood up, brushed back his hair, straightened his clothing as best he could, and sang two verses for the camera.

Dennis Watts flew into the county airport just past midnight with the preliminary autopsy report in his briefcase. The moon was bright enough so that he didn't call ahead to have the operator of the airport turn on the lights. It would have meant the operator had to drive all the way from town and Dennis enjoyed the challenge of drifting down, seeing the runway glowing in the moonlight and then feeling the first feathery touch of the landing gear and then the give of shocks and the solidity of a perfect landing. He used his key to get into the airport office and called Jug at home where Bessie told him that Jug was in town at the jail.

Once he saw the problem, Dennis tried a no nonsense approach. He marched up to the cell and said, "Now Burt, this has gone far enough. Just hand over the key." Burt grinned and started a new verse.

Outside in Jug's car Dennis told Jug the results of the autopsy. It hit Jug hard. Dennis turned on the overhead light and read the findings of the autopsy. Marian Powers had been killed by the injection of between ten and thirty milligrams of epinephrine. Jug moaned aloud.

"That poor lady died a horrible death," Dennis said. "You know how when you get a real scare the adrenaline shoots into your stomach with an almost painful spurt and you breath faster and get tense? Well, multiply that a million times. Whoever injected the fatal dose would have seen the results immediately. She would have gone pale, felt like vomiting. Her neck would have started hurting. Her breathing would have become labored, her muscles shaking, then the pain would have started in her heart and the heart would begin to run away, beating wildly and then she would have known and, probably, by that time, would not have even been able to scream."

"You're sure there's no way it could have been an accident?" Jug asked.

"No way. Anyone with the training of a nurse or a doctor, the only ones authorized to give her an injection, would have known it was an overdose."

Jug had been on his feet for a long time. He could see his political career flying away on the wings of Burt Scoggins' drinking song. He was tired. "Dennis, Lance Carver is out there. How about you go talk to him. The two of you work on it. Way I feel I wouldn't be any good and I'd sorta like to stay around here."

"I understand, Jug," Dennis said. "Don't worry about it. We'll handle it."

Jug went back inside. Just as Dennis drove away his primary opponent arrived in the company of two of the Swansey lawyers who were masterminding the campaign against him. Burt rose to the occasion and now the Republican alderman was familiar enough with the song to join Burt on the chorus.

And whenever he got loaded, you could hear him loudly bawl,
Oh, save the kids and women first, then save the al-key-hol

At the hospital things had settled down. Mrs. Lowery, the night supervisor, had called Mrs. Collins; and the cook and her helper, with the help of Deother Robinson, the night orderly, were cleaning up the kitchen. It had been relatively simple to establish the source of the copious quantities of blood which had been scattered arund the kitchen. Lowery had taken Lance down the hall to the lab and opened the door of a refrigerator.

"Just as I thought," she said. "There were six pints of whole blood there."

"How did you know about it?" Lance asked.

"I ordered it over from the blood bank on Dr. Kilgore's orders," Lowery said, "on Thursday night. That's when the auto accident happened?" Lance nodded. "Turned out it wasn't needed, after all, because the boy died before we could use it."

"This happen on the graveyard shift?"

"The rescue squad brought in the victims just after midnight," Lowery said. "I came down to emergency to help. It was hectic for a while. The rescue squad sent a man to the blood bank for it and got back with it just after one, too late."

"You don't ordinarily keep whole blood?"

"No. We don't have proper long term storage."

Lance sat at the desk at the fist-floor nurse's station and looked over his lists. There seemed to be a pattern to the incidents. They came either during the eleven-to-seven shift or around a shift change. Marian Powers' body had been moved in the middle of the shift. The breakfast tray had been switched at about the time of or shortly after the morning shift change, and the blood had been spilled in the kitchen around the time of the eleven o'clock shift change.

He concentrated, then, on the people authorized to be in the hospital from eleven at night until seven in the morning. On the first floor there were two registered nurses, Mrs. Lowery and Delphi Pond, along with the licensed practical nurse, Betty Mae Scoggins. Alice Perry, RN, was on duty in the emergency room with Dr. John King. On the second floor there were Mrs. Lorna Carpenter, a young registered nurse, and a nurse's aid, Mrs. Rachel Maddock. Deother Robinson, the nighttime orderly, shifted from floor to floor as needed.

Of all of them, Delphi Pond was the junior member in employment time, having been at Bellamy just under a year. Of Dr. John King, Lance found by talking with Lowery that he was not properly a member of the hospital staff. A lieutenant in the Marine Corp, he staffed the emergency room on weekends only, alternating weekends with another Marine doctor, both from the Marine base at Jacksonville. There were only three doctors in residence in Earlysburg. They alternated being on call for emergencies Monday through Thursday nights and the load was lifted from them Friday, Saturday, and Sunday nights by hiring the Marine doctors. King slept in the hospital in whatever room happened to be vacant.

Mrs. Scoggins, having finished her round of bedpan service, fixed Lance a cup of coffee. Lowery was working on paperwork. Delphi Pond had been making the rounds with a medication tray. She placed it on a shelf behind the station and sat down on the couch, crossing one shapely, white-clad leg over the other. The hospital had quieted down. Other than staff and patients there was a middle-aged housewife sitting up with her dying mother in room six.

"I know a little bit by now about the operation of the hospital," Lance said to Lowery, "but I wonder if things are quiet enough for you to take time to go around with me and explain where everything is and what it's for."

"Delphi, honey, would you do that?" Lowery asked. "I'm snowed under with paperwork."

Delphi smiled. "Where do you want to start?"

"Right here," Lance said. "I noticed that when you were taking medicines around you got them out of the cabinet there."

"Yes," Delphi said. "We know what medictions we'll need and we draw them from the main pharmacy in advance. We also keep some stock here in the cabinet, laxatives, antacids, things like that."

"Just common medicines, huh? No drugs?"

"Mainly just a supply of drugs currently prescribed for patients under present care," Delphi said.

"O.K., fine," Lance said. "Now let's go for a walk." He led the way down the hall into the patient wing. Delphi showed him the intensive care room, now vacant, and explained briefly the use of the array of equipment in the room. There was one vacant room on the lower floor. The rest had from one to three patients. At the back of the ell, Lance pushed the handle on the double doors and the door opened outward.

"This door locked from the outside?"

"Yes."

To test it he went out and let the door close. Delphi had to open it for him. "So you can go out but you can't come in unless you prop the door open." Outside the door was a cement ramp slanting down to a gravel walk. "They take the body out this door this morning?"

"Yes. Mr. Truval came in the front door and his body was waiting around back with a stretcher."

"Who gave Miss Powers the injection at three o'clock?" Lance asked.

"Mrs. Lowery. That was the only thing going at that time. Betty Mae and I were having a chat up at the nurse's station."

"She get sick immediately?"

"No, Lowery came back and sat down and it must have been, oh, five to ten minutes before the light came on in Miss Powers' room and I went down to find her in distress. I called Lowery and she called Dr. King up from emergency. He was, in fact, upstairs asleep and it took probably five minutes to get him there. Miss Powers was in great distress by that time and she died shortly after Dr. King came into the room. Then he spent about ten minutes trying to get her heart started again."

"Then what?"

"There was nothing else to do. Dr. King certified her as being dead and we covered her up and left her. Lowery called the funeral home. Dr. Epstein likes to get dead patients out of the hospital as soon as possible, but Mr. Truval was on call somewhere, so there was nothing to do but leave her there. We closed the door and went on back to the station and it wasn't more than, say, thirty minutes before Betty Mae went down to the kitchen for something and found her at the reception desk."

"Do you think someone could have carried her up the hall without being seen by any of you three?"

"No, I don't think so. I don't remember any time after she died that we were not at the station. Nothing else was going on."

"So to get her past the nurse's station someone had to carry her outside, around the building and in the front door."

"Or up the hall past Emergency."

"Where was the orderly during all this time?"

"He was around the room during the crisis, then he had a call from Mrs. Carpenter, upstairs. When things are slow he sometimes sneaks into a room and takes a nap. I didn't see him again until all the excitement early in the morning when Betty Mae found the body, then he came down after we'd moved the body back to the room."

Lance led the way back up the hall. "I know the offices and the kitchen," he said. "That door at the end of the hall is like the one back there? Locked from the outside?"

"Yes."

"So tell me about the rooms along the main hall," Lance said, turning toward Emergency.

"Linen supply on the right," she said, as they walked along. "Bathroom, the blood drawing lab and P.J.'s lab on the left. The X-Ray rooms, two of them. The Pharmacy."

"I've never seen anyone on duty in there," Lance said.

"No. We have keys. If we need something at night we take it and sign for it."

"Morphine, codeine, things like that?"

"Under lock and key. Things like that, anything with narcotic qualities, are locked in a steel cabinet in the Pharmacy. They are issued on prescription only and the pharmacist downtown has to come to the hospital to do it."

"No one here has a key?"

"No one. If a patient, say, is being given demerol for pain the pharmacist issues enough to the nurse on the floor to get the patient through the night. In an emergency, we have to call the pharmacist. That rarely happens, because we know during the day—the day shift—what's going to be needed at night and it's issued and put in the cabinet by the station."

"This may not have a thing to do with anything," Lance said, "it's just that while money used to be the root of all evil today it's drugs. Any trouble, ever, with drugs here in the hospital?"

"Any drugs missing you mean?" She shook her head. "No, not that I ever heard."

"And I'd imagine there's no great amount of them on hand here at any time, anyhow," Lance said.

"I'd think not."

Further down the hall there were two storage closets, the emergency room and the doors leading up the rear stairs to the second floor. Alice Perry, the emergency room RN, was at the desk in reception, feet out, reading a woman's magazine. She was a long-legged black woman with a small pot, age somewhere in the late thirties, Lance would have guessed.

"You entertaining the law?" Alice asked, grinning at Delphi.

"Giving him the grand tour," Delphi said.

"You got any idea who's been messing up this hospital?" Alice demanded.

"Have you?" Lance countered. He knew Alice Perry, of course. Her husband was a longshoreman at the depot and they lived in one of the better houses on the outskirts of the black section, a new four bedroom brick house with a big lawn.

"I had I'd kick me a little ass," Alice said, and the look on her face seemed to say that she could do it.

Lance walked into the treatment area and saw Dr. John King leaning over a desk on the front wall. King's head was down. Lance cleared his throat and King jerked erect, looked at Lance with his eyes going wide, then picked up a pen and made a notation on the paper in front of him. "Any luck?" he asked.

"Not yet." Lance said.

Delphi spoke to the doctor and then led Lance around the room past the three examining tables in their curtained enclosures and the array of machines—all under the harsh light of a dozen florescent fixtures in the ceiling. King watched them and then, as Lance started out, stood. "Guess I'll sneak off for a nap," he said, preceeding them out of the room.

"Two's empty," Delphi called after him.

"Yes, thank you."

In the hall Lance asked, "You said he was asleep upstairs last night?"

"Yes. Actually, it's quieter up there."

"Let's see how quiet it is tonight," Lance said. He pulled open one of the two doors leading to the stairwell.

"Those doors are supposed to stay locked," Delphi said. "But someone is always taping the lock." She pointed to the piece of white tape around the edge of the door which prevented the plunger from engaging when the door was closed. "Usually it's the doctors. They can come down the stairs and out the doors if they're called, but they can't get back in, and have to go all the way up the hall to the elevator. When I was on second floor I used to fuss at them about it. There are fewer rooms on second and it gets very, very quiet up there late at night. And anyone in the world could walk in the back door, which is always open—it's the emergency room entrance—and right up the stairs, and unless you're looking down the hall you'd never know they were up there. I had a woman in for tests and her husband kept sneaking up the stairs at night."

"For purposes of assaulting her honor?" Lance said, chuckling.

"Poor woman feeling so bad, but apparently she couldn't say no," Delphi said, laughing back at him. She showed a smooth and even set of white teeth when she smiled.

They walked down the hall, peering into the rooms. Lorna Carpenter, a small white girl of Delphi's size, was drinking coffee at the station. Grandmotherly Rachel Maddock, the black aide, was on the couch, knitting. Mrs. Carpenter had questions to ask about the incident in the kitchen. Lance asked more questions of his own. Neither the nurse nor the aide had seen anyone doing anything unusual during the evening.

Doether Robinson was sleeping in an empty room near the second-floor nurse's station. He did not stir when Lance looked into the room. The operating room was empty and cold-looking. There was a linen storage and a room used for storage of odd equipment. Aside from the baths in the patients' rooms, there was a bath with shower on the front hall.

Overall, Bellamy was in the shape of an F, with the long side toward Water Street and the westernmost wing a bit shorter than the middle bar of the F. Originally, the building had been in the shape of a T, consisting of the front portion and the wing extending back to Emergency. Later additions to the first floor had added patients' room on the western ell and the kitchen to the eastern end of the lower floor. There were entrances to the lower floor at each wing end, a total of four. Access to the second floor was by the stairwell across from the emergency room, by elevator and by the front stairs across from the administration offices.

Now Lance was familiar with the layout and he had all of the names straight in his mind. Thinking about it as he and Delphi rode down in the elevator, the nice smell of her mild scent in his nostrils, he couldn't see any of the hospital employees pulling the grotesque pranks. What was the motive? There were, of course, many more people to be taken into consideration, the three-to-eleven shift, the seven-to-three shift, all of the office and lab workers who were present in the hospital during the day. He had now talked with everyone who worked the graveyard shift, however, and none of them had noticed anyone who didn't belong on the night shift. The night shift was, collectively, the prime suspect, but there was always the possibility of the "dirty deeds" having been done by a complete outsider. There just wasn't a helluva lot he could do short of hanging around and hoping that the prankster would strike again under more controlled circumstances, for example, that night, when he knew how many people were in the place down to and including the woman spending the night sitting up with her sick mother.

He had little faith in the prankster. It would take a real fool to try another trick with the fuzz right there in the joint. Delphi got them coffee once they had reached the first-floor station where Lowery was going at her knitting in a calm frenzy, and Betty Mae was reading. Then Dennis Watts came in, pulled Lance aside up into the lobby and hit him with the news. Now it was murder and not just mean tricks.

"I think we'd better get Jug out here," Lance said shaken.

"Jug's got problems of his own," Dennis said, explaining the crisis at the jail. "There's not much can be done tonight except hang around and observe the routine. I think it would be best if we didn't let it out that we know the woman was deliberately overdosed." Dennis then outlined his new knowledge of the drug epinephrine, how it was usually administered in a weak solution in small quantities, how it would have taken a very large dose, larger than was practical, to kill the woman using the ordinary ampules. "I'd say look for a different solution, one prepared for inhalation instead of injection. Is there anyone here you trust enough to sort of hint around and find out if there's such a solution in the hospital?"

"I know most of them from seeing them around town, and some of them well," Lance said. "I'll feel around a little."

"I'd stay if there was anything I could do," Dennis said, "but it might just make someone suspicious if both of us were prowling around."

"I dig," Lance said. He returned to the nurse's station and sat next to Delphi on the couch. He did not start his questions immediately. She talked about how she'd been on the floor while he was in with his gunshot wound. Lance said he sure did appreciate all the good care he got. She asked him if the wound still bothered him and he said only when it was going to rain. The night grew older slowly. Betty Mae Scoggins turned a transister radio to an all night FM station, the music low and soft. Lance smoked too much and got Delphi talking about herself. She was a county girl, went to high school at the western end of the county, got a degree in English and an associate degree in nursing after two years of training. She hoped to write someday.

"And what about you?" she asked. "What do you do other than drive around in a sheriff's car?"

"As little as possible," Lance said. "I dig music, like to go to the beach."

"Gosh, I haven't been to the beach this year," Delphi said, looking at him with wide eyes. He let it pass. He started asking her about her work, about strange cases and various things that a nurse had to do. She talked easily and interestingly.

"I guess I'll never get hardened to it," she said, talking about a child who had died two weeks past. "They say you do. They say you can't afford to get emotionally involved with the patients or you'll go crazy. I love it when a patient comes in in pain or very ill and we, the doctors, make him well and send him on his own two feet, but there's always the other possibility. There are always those who come in and then are carried out the back door by Mr. Truval."

"Guess a nurse has a lot of responsibility," Lance said, just to keep her primed and talking.

"Well, we have to know a lot of emergency procedures. We have to know a little bit of what a doctor knows. I can start a stopped heart if I have to. Did it once. Actually, aside from actual surgery, the doctor finds the problem and gives orders and it's the nurse who does the actual healing, if you want to put it that way. We are responsible for medications on doctor's orders. We are responsible for keeping an eye on the patient's condition. The doctor sees the patient twice a day. We see him many times."

"Guess you have to know a lot about drugs and medicines," Lance said.

"Oh, yes, Mistakes can happen, a doctor can be tired. He can write down the wrong thing. We're responsible for knowing which drugs are used in a particular course of treatment and the amounts usually given. Time and time again a good nurse has saved a patient from an overdose or a wrong medicine. If there's any doubt in your mind you go back and ask the doctor if that's what he meant. Any doctor worth his salt won't object. He'll appreciate being checked on and he expects it. And then, too, doctors' handwriting is a standard joke."

"Take the woman who died," Lance said. "Any possibility of her being given an overdose?"

"Oh, no," Delphi said. "Epinephrine comes in an ampule of the proper size for the dose. The worst that could have happened is that one ampule would be substituted for the other, but it would have been a difference of no more than three-tenths of a cc."

"I'm getting sleepy," Lance said. "Why don't you and I take a little walk."

"All right."

They walked down the main hall and turned toward the rear of the hospital. Lance put a quarter in the coke machine. Delphi didn't want a drink.

"This stuff, this epi—"

"Epinephrine. Why do you keep coming back to it?"

"Just wondering," Lance said, "if it's in the hospital in any other form, like in a stronger solution, say for inhalation treatment."

Delphi looked at him sharply. "You do have a reason for asking, don't you?"

"Just want to set the record straight."

"It's possible. I'm not sure."

"Could we check?"

"It would be in the Pharmacy. The key is back at the station."

"Why don't you run and get it?" He put his hand on her arm. "Get it without the others seeing you if you can."

"You know, you're beginning to scare me." But she went, her hips swaying under the neat uniform. Lance chugged the coke and put the bottle in the rack and then she was back. She unlocked the door and turned on the lights.

"The quickest way is to check inventory," she said. She opened a drawer and pulled out a spiral notebook. "Anyone who takes medication out is supposed to enter it. Sometimes someone is in a hurry and forgets, but we'll be able to see if there's ever been any, or if there is any now, from the sheets." She thumbed through the book. "Yes, here we are. 'U.S.P. Epinephrine Solution 1:100.'" She moved her face closer to the book, as if doing a double take. " 'U.S.P. Epinephrine Solution 1:10' " She looked up. "Both for use in a special nebulizer to provide a fine mist for inhalation. The one to ten is very strong. I've never seen it before, but then I've had no occasion to be in on treating a patient by inhalation. How did you know?"

"Been doing my homework," Lance said. "Let's find the stuff."

The one to one hundred solution was on a top shelf. Delphi took down the bottle and shook it. There was sediment in the bottom and some brownish discoloration. "This has been here too long," she said.

The stronger solution, the ten to one, was not in evidence. Delphi searched the entire shelf area without finding it. "As I say," she said, "someone could have taken it without taking it off the inventory list."

But Lance was thinking differently. He was thinking about garbage. He thought it was unlikely that the city had made a pickup since the morning. Somewhere in the hospital or in the immediate vicinity, perhaps in one of the large bins at the back, Lance was sure he'd find a container for epinephrine.

There was nothing he could do during the night, however. He went back to the nurse's station with Delphi, had a cup of coffee and watched the night creep past slowly. Now and then there'd be a call from a patient, but mostly the night staff read, knitted, or dozed in a chair. Lance himself dozed from six to just before seven and the prankster had not struck again. He stayed through the shift change. The offices were not open on Sunday nor were the labs. He left at seven-thirty with the hospital taking on a quiet early morning bustle and was asleep in his own bed within a half hour.

Chapter Eight

Jug knew it was all over by eleven o'clock Sunday morning. Popeye, the local reporter, had been allowed to take his pictures and run off to send his feature story about a sheriff being locked out of his own jail to the AP. Half the county, it seemed, had visited. The jail had never been so popular. Inside the cell, the level in the last tall coke bottle was getting low.

"Burt," Jug said, feeling just a little sad, "I've been in law enforcement in this county for almost forty-five years. I've been sheriff for thirty of those years and I never yet took a drink on duty."

Burt stopped singing. His voice was getting tired and he was beginning to feel a little funny. The way Jug was talking, the tone of his voice, it sounded as if it were important. Jug got up and walked around a couple of the smart-assed young lawyers and got a clean but chipped mug down off the shelf and passed it through the bars to Burt. Burt poured generously. Jug drank slowly, remembering all the years. He'd go on running. A man doesn't quit when the going gets tough, but he knew enough about politics to know that being made a fool of is one of the surest ways of getting whupped in an election. It's sometimes easier to laugh a man out of office than it is to beat him with the logic of democracy.

Dodo, meanwhile, had been sleeping it off on his cot alongside the wall. His snores and snorts and a couple of fairly entertaining nightmares, during which he acted a lot like a dog chasing rabbits in his sleep, made the night pass away faster for those who alternated watching Burt perform with Jug. Along about churchtime Dodo woke up and ran to the toilet and was violently sick. He looked bad. He complained about stomach pain and couldn't keep down the coffee Jug fixed for him.

Burt himself was beginning to hurt. Both he and Dodo had consumed prodigious amounts of pure corn, and Burt had been soaking his insides in it for over twenty-four hours.

"I'm afraid the old man has been poisoned by that stuff," Alderman Gillette said. "No telling what's in it, lead, lye, who knows?"

"It was a good still," Jug said. "No old car radiators or anything like that. Good copper tubing and good procedures. He may have had too much, but he ain't poisoned." He had just finished a drink of it himself, and it was fine corn. Besides, he knew the moonshiner and knew for a fact that the man took pride in making a good, clean product.

But Dodo was in a bad way. He was hugging his stomach and moaning. Jug called the town rescue squad to come and take Dodo out to the hospital so the doctor could take a look at him. Burt, concerned, was standing by the cell door. He had to hang onto the bars. The world was going alternately red and black on him. Dodo let out a particularly loud groan and it hurt Burt so badly that he chugged a good ounce of the corn and then, with a smile on his face, sank down limply to life in a crumpled heap near the cell door. Jug leaned over and reached in and fished the key out of his pocket. When the rescue squad ambulance came he loaded both Burt and Dodo in it and followed it to the hospital.

They put another bed in room two and within a few minutes both Burt and Dodo were taking glucose and liquids intravenously.

Jug was dead on his feet. He walked back up the hall, after seeing Burt and Dodo safely in bed, and stopped at the nurse's station to ask if his deputy, Lance Carver, had been around. The nurse there told him that Lance was, or had been, in the hospital with P.J. Charlie. Jug wandered around a little and finally spotted Lance and P.J. out back leaning over the garbage bins.

Lance had drafted P.J., over many objections, to help him make a search for the missing container of epinephrine. Lance had supplied old cotton gloves, but that wasn't keeping all the soggy contents of the garbage bins from smelling to high heaven. P.J. was complaining about how he'd gone to school to learn to be a professional man and not a garbage man, and Lance was telling him to shut up and keep digging. Lance had gone home to get a quick breakfast and about three hours sleep, and he wasn't enjoying the digging either.

Jug watched, unseen, for a few minutes and then he cleared his throat. Lance straightened up, holding his soggy hands out, and grinned at Jug. "We could use all the help we can get," he said.

"Boy, I learned a long time ago how to delegate responsibility," Jug said. "Although I'm not sure what responsibility this is, digging around in the trash."

Lance told him the situation and Jug agreed that

it was a good idea to try to find the missing container. He was too tired to be shocked by having the pranks at the hospital turn into possible murder. He told Lance to call and wake him if the container was found.

"You might look in now and then on Burt and Dodo, too," Jug said. "Damned fool might wake up and try to go off looking for a drink."

The two large bins yielded nothing. Lance and P.J. Charlie went inside, washed in the hall bath, had a coke and discussed possibilities. P.J. suggested that they get Jimbo Rogers, the orderly, in on the search. "They 'bout a million hiding places in this old building," P.J. said.

P.J. called Jimbo and Lance told him what they were looking for and cautioned him to keep the search as secret as possible. Jimbo's eyes widened, and he got into the spirit of things. They began in the emergency room. Only a nurse was there, Dr. King was upstairs taking a nap. Then they worked their way up the hall, looking in all rooms, checking all waste baskets, nooks and corners.

Jimbo made the first find. The waste basket in the visitors bath downstairs hadn't been emptied since Friday. He came out and caught up with Lance and P.J. Charlie as they were checking the waste basket near the receptionist's desk. "This may not mean nothin'," he said, "but it hadn't oughta been there."

He held a piece of tissue with blood spots and the cap from a drug ampule. Lance shrugged. "So?"

"I say it may not mean nothin'. It's just the top off an ampule, like you take off the cap and stick the needle in and fill it. The tissue looks to me like it's been used to dab the blood off the needle hole in someone's arm."

Lance took the two items and put them into an envelope from the office. Jimbo found exactly the same thing in the waste basket in room two, where Dodo and Burt were sleeping peacefully, glucose running slowly into their systems to counteract the alcohol.

"Someone's been shooting up sure as hell," P.J. Charlie said.

"Let's keep this between us," Lance said, "for the time being."

"You fuzz," Jimbo said, "but you a brother. I keep quiet." P.J. Charlie nodded.

The upstairs hall bath yielded still another ampule top and a piece of blooded tissue. The afternoon shift was coming on. Jimbo went off home. Lance and P.J. Charlie spent another three hours in a search of odd corners of the hospital without results. Then they went to the Waterfront Restaurant for a well-earned seafood platter, Lance springing for the check.

Lance thought about the situation for a full thirty seconds after he hit his bed, and then he was awakened by the alarm. He put on a clean uniform, after showering, and went to the hospital.

Since he had already taken Delphi partially into his confidence he chose her to ask about the ampule tops. He looked at them and turned toward the medicine cabinet behind the desk. They were alone, Mrs. Lowery having answered a room call and Betty Mae also off toward the end of the hall somewhere. Delphi searched for a moment and then turned to him, frowning.

"I thought I could show you a full ampule," she said. "We had several here the last time I did an inventory."

"Ask about it," Lance said, seeing Lowery coming back up the hall.

"Mrs. Lowery, have you had a patient on Benadryl lately?" Delphi asked.

"Not in the past few weeks," Lowery said. "Why?"

"What's Benadryl?" Lance said quickly.

"It's an anthihistamine," Lowery said. "Used in the treatment of asthma and some allergies. Ever take a seasick pill?"

"I've got a cast iron stomach," Lance said.

"A neutralized form of Benadryl is used in Dramamine, the seasick pill," Lowery said. "It also has a moderate antispasmodic action in the Benadryl Hydrochloride form."

"The caps are definitely from Benadryl?" Lance asked.

"Yes," both Delphi and Lowery said.

"And it's not a drug. I mean it wouldn't be locked up in the drug cabinet?"

"Almost anything can be misused," Lowery said. "In large doses Benadryl has a sedative effect."

"Like a downer," Delphi said.

"But someone would have to be damned stupid to take that much of it," Lowery said.

"Or that desperate," Delphi said.

"If someone were shooting this stuff could you tell by looking at him?" Lance said. "I mean, enlarged pupils or something like that?"

"I actually don't know," Lowery said. "He'd be loggy and sleepy if he had enough of it."

Delphi laughed. "Everyone on the night shift acts that way at times."

"Del, let's me and you take another trip to the Pharmacy," Lance said. She got the key and he walked beside her. Once she brushed against him and he was aware of the solid girl underneath the slickness of her white uniform.

After checking the inventory book Delphi said, "We should have twenty ampules of fifty mg."

The shelves, as Lance expected, yielded nothing. He asked Delphi to come with him and went upstairs. Lorna Carpenter was seated at the desk doing paperwork.

"How's your stock of Benadryl?" Delphi asked. "We've had a run on it."

Mrs. Carpenter did not look up. "Yes, just a minute." She finished making a notation and asked, "How much do you need?"

"Two fifty mg ampules will get us through the night," Delphi said.

Lorna Carpenter went to the medicine cabinet and used her key to open it. She looked inside for a moment. "Well," she said, "we seem to be out, too."

"That's strange," Delphi said.

"Yes, isn't it?" Lorna sat down. "Sorry. You did try the Pharmacy I suppose."

"Twenty ampules have been taken without being removed from the inventory sheet," Delphi said.

"Well, you know how it is, people get busy and forget," Lorna said.

"What about the ampules in your cabinet," Lance said, "any idea what happened to them?"

"No."

"If there had been a patient on Benadryl wouldn't you know? I mean, they wouldn't be given the drug just during the day would they?"

"Possibly," Lorna said. "And perhaps someone from emergency came and got ours for out-patient use. If you're desperate for it, Del, call the pharmacist and have him bring some. He's paid to keep our stock in order."

"Yes, fine," Delphi said.

In the elevator Lance asked, "Is she always like that?"

"She's just a little red-necked," Delphi said, "and a little more weird."

"How weird?"

"Well, it has nothing to do with you," Delphi said.

"How do you know?"

"Look, we're a lot like a little family out here. We don't like to tattle on each other."

"Won't tell," Lance said, grinning and crossing his heart.

"I still don't think it's any of your business," she said, "but she shot up insulin."

"That's for diabetes."

"Yes, but she had a different disease."

"Quit being coy," Lance said as the elevator door opened.

Delphi stepped out. "She was having marital problems. I guess she just wanted some attention."

"She doesn't have diabetes, then."

"No."

"What happens when a normal person takes insulin, then?"

"Well, insulin metabolizes carbohydrates. It lowered her blood sugar. She was weak and pale and having funny symptoms."

"Why would she deliberately make herself ill?"

"I said she was having family problems. Do you know Don Carpenter?"

"I know him."

"He hasn't worked now in over a year," Delphi said. "He's been in trouble a couple of times—"

"Nothing serious," Lance said. "DWI once and once a bust for a minor amount of grass."

"Lorna wants a divorce and he won't cooperate."

"This day and time all she has to do is go to a lawyer." He knew. He hadn't wanted a divorce, either, but before she was killed Glenda was going through the first stage of getting one.

"I think, and this is pure speculation on my part, that she's in love."

"Who with?"

"Are you just being curious?"

"No," he said.

"Dr. King."

"So?"

"The three times it happened, was on weekends while he was on duty."

"She shot up insulin three times?"

"Last time she almost overdid it. That's when he found out what she was doing. She collapsed on duty and went into a coma. He did all he could and it was enough to pull her through. He's a very good doctor."

"How long ago was this?"

"Oh, three or four months. Dr. King made her go see a psychiatrist. He discussed her with Dr. Eptstein and they decided that if she'd get help they'd let her keep her job. She's all right now. Or seems to be."

"And you think she took the insulin just to get attention from Dr. King?" Lance asked.

"I said that was just speculation on my part."

"Any evidence of anything between them?"

"No, not really."

"What does not really mean?"

"Well, definitely not here in the hospital."

"How can you know for sure? The door to the second floor is taped open. It gets quiet here at night."

"You have a dirty mind," she said.

"People do strange things. You said not really."

"Well, one night when we went off duty, Dr. King asked me if I'd like to have a midnight snack with him and just as we were going out Lorna came down and he asked her to go with us. I thought it was sort of strange, although he is a Yankee, for him to ask me, you know?"

"We still don't do it in technicolor in Earlysburg," Lance said. "Yes."

"I got the idea, after we got down to the tavern, down by the river, you know? I got the idea that I was there as a chaperon. Oh, they included me in the conversation, but they didn't object at all when I said I had to go. I'd followed them there in my own car, so I left them there."

"Was this before or after she shot up the insulin?"

"In between times, if I remember right."

"So maybe she did get his attention with her little ruse, huh?"

"I don't think this has a thing to do with what you're here for," she said, turning to walk away.

He followed. "Del, hold it a minute." She halted and looked up at him. There was something in her eyes which made him a little uncomfortable. She was expecting something other than the surprise he had for her and he was, for a moment, sorry he couldn't give it to her. Then the empty feeling in his gut returned.

"Del, Marian Powers was overdosed."

"What?"

"A massive overdose. It almost had to be deliberate."

"Oh, God," she said. "Who?"

"That's what I have to find out. Now I want you to think very carefully. So far there's only one man who seems to have any kind of motive for killing Miss Powers, and I can't swallow Dr. Epstein as a serious suspect."

"I should think not," she said, her eyes flaring.

"You think about it. Any other strange little incidents involving staff, things like Lorna Carpenter shooting insulin?"

"No," she said quickly. "I mean, I'll think about it, but I think no."

Chapter Nine

"What I want to know," Betty Mae Scoggins was saying to Lowery, "is who pays. He's put in here by the county, coming from the county jail. Don't that make him county responsibility?"

"I'd think so," Lowery said.

"Because I had to let the health insurance drop. Me, I get a reduced rate if I get sick and the kids have school insurance. They promised Burt they was getting insurance on his job, but it won't come in for a while yet and I'm not sure it would cover sobering up anyhow."

"I wouldn't worry about it, Betty Mae," Lowery said.

"It's hard enough to pay the electricity, what with it going up and up," Betty Mae said. "And with Burt blowing half his pay." She sniffed and wiped her nose with her handkerchief. "And he'd been so good the past few weeks."

"I'm sure the county will pay, since he got the stuff in Jug Watson's jail," Lowery said. "Now you stop worrying and go down and see if the IV's are finished on those two scoundrels."

The bottles were empty. Although she wasn't supposed to do it, she'd done more than that that she wasn't supposed to do during her years as a licensed practical nurse, so she pulled the needles out of Burt's arm first and then Dodo's and swabbed down the wounds with alochol and saw that they were not bleeding. Burt was sleeping noisily, making snorts and grunts through his nose. She watched him for a few minutes, sitting on the edge of his bed. Burt wasn't a bad man, it was just that he had his weakness. And, God, he'd been a scamp when he was young and she was young. She removed the IV stands and put them in the equipment room and checked doors as she went back up the hall. It was quiet after midnight.

Lance made a quiet tour of the hospital. Lowery and Delphi had finished their early duties and were settled down at the nurse's station. All was peaceful. Deother, the orderly, was sacked out in an upstairs room. Dr. King was in the other empty room on the second floor. Lorna Carpenter gave him a brief smile as he walked past her desk. The second-floor aide, Mrs. Maddock, was knitting again.

He went down the rear stairs, noting that the lock on the door was still taped open. He was standing in front of the coke machine, considering whether or not to put another few ounces of sweetened water into his stomach, when he heard the siren coming far down the street. He knew the sound of the Fortier Beach rescue squad ambulance and he walked back to Emergency and looked out the back door. Alice Perry joined him there. The ambulance wheeled into the emergency entrance, lights flashing.

"Lance, honey," Alice Perry said, "would you run up and wake Dr. King?"

There was an urgency in the movements of the men who leaped from the front seat of the ambulance. A car squealed turning its tires into the emergency entrance behind the ambulance. Lance took the stairs two at a time. He stood in the open door and turned on the light. King was sleeping on his back, fully clothed. Lance called him by name. Excited voices and assorted banging sounds came up the stairwell from below. King did not move. Lance shook him, hand on his shoulder. King groaned and tried to turn over, and Lance was saying, "Dr. King."

King opened his eyes and lifted his head, it nodding weakly for a moment before he groaned again and put his hand on his neck.

"Emergency downstairs," Lance said, "are you all right?"

"Huh?" King squinted his eyes in the light and turned his head sideways to look at Lance. "Yes, thank you."

Lance was back downstairs for the entry of the second stretcher from the ambulance. He recognized the face of an Earlysburg teenager. The two men bringing in the stretcher were members of the Fortier Beach rescue squad, a store owner and the town maintenance man. "How bad?" Lance asked.

"He's tore up inside," the maintenance man said.

King came down, pulling his white smock. His hair was mussed and he looked very tired. Alice Perry, the two stretcher cases inside, was shooing out the rescue squad members. There were six of them, some having followed the ambulance in the car. Lance asked the maintenance man what had happened.

"The kid was running from the cops. Went into this other car head on in front of Jack's store."

Alice Perry stuck her head out the door. "Lance, would you go up and send Lowery down here? We're going to need all the help we can get."

Lance loped up the hall and Lowery came on the

run. He talked with the rescue squad members. The Fortier Beach night man came in and they compared notes on the accident, fuzz to fuzz. There'd be charges against the Earlysburg teenager.

"If that man dies," the Fortier Beach policeman said, "it'll be manslaughter if I have my way. I clocked the little bastard at ninety-eight."

There was something akin to a party atmosphere in the hall outside the emergency room. Lance had noted it before. It wasn't meant to be disrespectful. They were good people and they led quiet, unexciting lives and when something dramatic happened the adrenalin flowed and talk was animated and there was a lot of smoking.

It was almost a half hour before Alice Perry came out of the treatment room. She looked beat. She stood in the hall doorway and looked at them for a second. "Tommy's dead," she said. "There was nothing we could do."

"No charges," the Fortier Beach policeman said. Tommy was the teenager.

"How about the other fellow?" a member of the squad asked.

"Broken ribs and right arm, concussion," Perry said. "He'll make it."

The rescue squad drifted away back to their beds and their quiet lives. Lance gave the Fortier Beach policeman a "see you later." Lowery came to the door and asked him to go up and tell Delphi that she'd be tied up helping in the emergency room for another hour.

Lance didn't mind being errand boy. It gave him something to do. He found Delphi at the desk and delivered the message. Betty Mae had just been down to see Burt again. He was still sleeping. Lance sat down. Delphi was doing the nightly paperwork. He smoked a cigarette and thought about things. It seemed as if he'd been hanging around the hospital forever and he'd only spent one night and part of another there. It seemed futile to hang around, but he had his orders. He tried to think of something positive he could do and thought of Lorna Carpenter. He walked up the front stairs to the second floor. Lorna was alone at the desk, doing nothing, staring straight ahead when he came quietly into the area. When she saw him she flashed her brief smile.

"All alone?" he asked.

"They drafted Deother and Mrs. Maddock to help clean up downstairs," she said. "They say Tommy Smith is dead."

"I'm afraid so."

"That's terrible, just terrible."

"It happens when you put a kid in a high-powered sports car," Lance said. He cleared his throat. There was no good way to bring up the subject. "Mrs. Carpenter, I've been wanting a chance to talk with you."

"About what's been going on in the hospital?"

"That's right. We think it's all connected with someone taking drugs."

"I can't believe that," she said.

"Well, where is all the Benadryl?"

"Benadryl is not a drug," she said.

"Only when misused, then it has a sedative effect. If someone were hooked on something else and couldn't get it, the sedative would lessen the withdrawal symptoms."

"Well, it's not really my affair, is it?"

"I'm afraid it's as much your's as anyone's," he said. "We'll have to ask you what happened to the Benadryl from your cabinet."

"Now look," she said, eyes flashing, "there are two other shifts on this floor. You'll have to ask them, too."

"But all of the incidents have happened during or just before or after the graveyard shift," Lance said. "Wouldn't you say the people on the late shift would be a good place to start asking questions?"

She picked up a pen and began to turn it end for end, tapping the desk top.

"I hate to bring this up, Mrs. Carpenter, but you seem to have a little experience with unauthorized injections." He watched her reaction closely. Her face went taut.

"Not drugs," she said.

"No." He waited her out, looking at her quietly, seriously.

"I've been punished enough for that moment of weakness," she said. She was such a pretty girl, Lance was thinking, delicate, well figured, small, her voice soft and hinting of a quality of intimacy.

"No one is talking about punishment," Lance said. "This little chat isn't even on the record. But when the full investigation starts you can expect some much rougher questions, I'm afraid. They're going to ask you about your relationship to Dr. King—"

She went white. "You have no right," she said. "You can't come in here when I'm on duty and accuse me—"

"Hey," he said. "No accusations, O.K.? I wish you'd just talk to me and not get excited."

"There is nothing between me and Dr. King," she said.

"Any idea what happened to the Benadryl?" Lance asked, to jar her.

"No, damn it, no."

"Did you ever have occasion to treat a patient with epinephrine by inhalation?"

She looked at him with a puzzled frown. "Once in nurses training I watched it."

"Never here in the hospital?"

"No."

"I understand you're having problems in your marriage."

She stood suddenly. "That's none of your business, you black sonofabitch."

"It's the color of the uniform that counts," Lance said calmly. "Sit down." He made his voice heavy. "Lorna, the fur is going to fly around here and soon. A woman's been murdered and we'll be tearing this place apart. What you're getting from me is just a sample, because you're in it. You're in it because you stepped across the line. Maybe you just did it once and maybe you had good reason, but you did and when there's a murder investigation on we pay special attention to people who have shown signs of antisocial behavior. Now I know your antisocial act was directed against yourself but it shows that something is bugging you and bugging you bad and we'll have to know what."

"You said a woman was murdered," she said, her voice weak.

"A deliberate overdose of epinephrine."

"Miss Powers? Oh, God."

"You wanta say anything about that?"

"You can't believe I had anything to do with it?"

He shrugged. "Someone with a knowledge of medicine did it."

"I was never even down there."

Lance lit a cigarette and pulled a chair up in

front of the desk. "Mrs. Carpenter, I may be wrong, but I think there's something you're not telling me."

"May I have one of those?" she asked. He handed her a cigarette and lit it. "All right," she said. "I gave Dr. King three ampules of 50 mg Benadryl." Her hand was shaking as she took a deep drag on the cigarette. "He said he wanted it for a friend of his who had an allergy. He offered to pay for it but I said the red tape involved wasn't worth it. He asked for more and there wasn't any left up here."

"When was that?"

"Last weekend, Saturday night."

"Was that the first time?"

"Yes. Dr. King doesn't have much to say to me."

"Oh?"

"I know what you're thinking. I know what they are saying, but it's not true. I simply wanted to die, that's all. I wasn't trying to get his attention. I was having problems with Don. I was feeling bad. I thought how wonderful it would be just to go to sleep, to slip into a coma and never wake up."

"Look, I'm sorry," Lance said. "I really am."

"I don't need your pity. I'm all right now."

Lance was feeling uncomfortable, but it was true that she would have to be questioned sooner or later. "Mrs. Carpenter, was there ever anything between you and Dr. King?"

"No."

"Would you say he is close to anyone else in the hospital?"

"Not that I know of. He's in constant pain, you know."

"No, I didn't know. What's wrong?"

"He doesn't talk about it, I know. As a nurse I can see he's in pain. I imagine it has to do with the accident, the scars on his neck."

"What sort of accident?" Lance asked.

"All he would ever say about it was, 'They almost got me.'"

"But the scars seem to be healed. Why should he still have pain?"

"There are different kinds of pain," she said.

"Explain that."

"It would be mere speculation," she said.

"Then speculate. As I said, this is off the record."

"He would never kill anyone," she said.

"I'm not accusing him."

"It's not unknown for a doctor to get hooked," she said.

"Is he hooked?"

"I didn't even suspect when he asked for the Benadryl, or I wouldn't have given it to him. It was only after you and Del came up asking about it that I looked it up in the book and I'd forgotten that Benadryl can be used as a downer." She stubbed out the cigarette. "Suppose he had a long hospitalization. Some of the pain killers can be addictive when used over a long period of time. Demerol can create a dependence, and if there's pain as an aftermath of the hospitalization, well, a doctor can get drugs, up to a certain point. It's one of the dangers of the profession."

"So you think it's possible that Dr. King is hooked on some drug, and is using the Benadryl?"

"I've been watching him. I've come upon him when he's alone, say in the office. He'll be sitting there, head down, and then when someone walks in he'll look up and pretend to be busy."

"How about checking your inventory sheet to see how many ampules of Benadryl are supposed to be in your cabinet."

"I did," she said. "We were issued twenty ampules."

"How long ago?"

"About six weeks."

"So it's been disappearing for some weeks now?"

"I can't say. It's seldom used. No one would notice it being missing unless there was a doctor's order for it and there wasn't any on the shelf."

"Dr. King," Lance said, "how long has he been working at the hospital?"

"About a year, but there was a period of about two months when he was hospitalized."

"And he came back to work about six weeks ago," Lance said. She nodded grimly.

"Mrs. Carpenter, it's possible that Jug or someone else might want to talk with you. I'll try to see to it that you're not bothered, but—"

"What the hell does it matter?" she asked bitterly. "Everyone in the whole damned hospital knows, why shouldn't we tell the world?"

Lance went down to the coke machine and punched out a drink. He was beginning to see a pattern. Dr. King had come back to work about six weeks ago and Benadryl had started disappearing and there was a considerable amount of it in the hospital. After six weeks the supply would have been getting low. The drug cabinet was locked and only the pharmacist downtown had a key, so harder drugs were not within easy access. Suppose that King had raided the pharmacy for all of the Benadryl there. The only ampules left were in the cabinets at the nurse's stations. Why not create a diversion to allow access to it? Miss Powers' body moved into the reception area had successfully drawn off all three of the first floor nurses for a long period of time. The serving of a grisly breakfast on the second floor had occupied the attentions of the whole hospital and now there was no Benadryl upstairs. The blood in the kitchen? A diversion to allow one last raid on the pharmacy? Everyone from emergency room staff on down had gathered there to take a look at the mess.

As he stood drinking the soft drink Dr. King came out of emergency, shedding his white coat, and went up the stairs. Lance considered tackling him. He decided to wait. He'd want to talk to Jug before he started accusing a doctor of drug addiction, petty theft, and perhaps much worse. He looked at his watch. Just past two in the morning, an awful time. Only two reasons to stay up that late that were worthwhile, booze and music, and booze and a woman. And thinking that way sent a slow sadness through him, because the first image which came to his mind was the face of Delphi Pond and the second was Glenda, with her stomach opened and spilling dark and arcane things.

The rescue squad ambulance, siren screaming, had passed fifty feet from the open window of room two, waking Burt to a living hell. He had never felt so bad in his life. He needed a cold beer, can glistening with moisture, the hiss of release as he popped the cap, the golden flow down his gullet to quiet the fires below. He couldn't even figure out where he was for a long time. He looked for the bars and they weren't there. The light was dim. There was another bed in the room. There was a white head on the pillow of the other bed.

It was the way he felt which gave him the first

clue. He'd been dried out forceably once or twice before and it was a feeling he recognized, people pumping all that damned sugar into his blood making him feel like a sugar bowl with a fire in it. He groaned and Dodo sat up suddenly saying, "What, what?"

"It's me, Burt," Burt said. "It's all right. They got us in the hospital, that's all."

"Are we sick?" Dodo asked. Then he groaned. "God, I'm sick."

"I'd have to get better to die," Burt confessed.

"Why we in the hospital, Burt?" Dodo asked, his head still messed up.

"They done dried us out," Burt said. "They done wasted all that good corn by feeding us sugar in the veins."

"An' me trying to lose weight," Dodo said. "Using saccharine in my coffee and all."

"It's a terrible thing to do to a man, Dodo," Burt said. "That hadn't oughta done that to us."

"Burt, I cain't remember nothin'," Dodo said. "Why ain't you in the cell?"

"That's not the problem," Burt said. "The problem is they ruined a lot of real good corn for us and me having decided, back there in the cell with it being so good, that it was my last time. Now they done cut my last time short and me getting ready to join the AA come Monday."

The more he thought about it the more unfair it seemed. He was ready to get out of the bed and tell them what he thought of people who would deliberately ruin a man's last drunk, the best drunk a man had ever had, with a good audience and him remembering all the verses he'd ever thought up and coming up with a few new ones. It would serve them right.

But then he had a more brilliant idea. It came to him slowly because he had a headache, but it came. He was in the hospital. P.J. Charlie worked at the hospital and many's the time he'd had a swig out of P.J. Charlie's plastic jug. P.J. Charlie liberated medical alcohol from the hospital, and it was almost as strong, maybe stronger than good corn. P.J. Charlie, Burt knew from talking with his wife, worked in the lab. That's where the alcohol would be.

"Dodo," Burt said, "they done a terrible thing to us, are we gonna take it lying down?"

"No." A pause. "What we gonna do about it?"

"They cut off the best drunk two men ever had," Burt said. "We can't allow them to do that, not with me joining AA on Monday."

"Don't see much we can do," Dodo said. "It's night out. Looks like it's late."

"Dodo, do you feel as bad as I do?"

"I feel pretty bad."

"Do you feel like if you could have just one little taste of something it might help?"

Dodo smacked his lips, thinking about it, the hair of the dog they called it.

"I just happen to know where we can get us a little taste."

"My God," Dodo said, "where?"

"Right here in the hospital. You game?"

"I think I'm gonna die," Dodo said.

Burt got out of bed. "Come on," he said, pulling Dodo up. Dodo stood unsteadily and looked down at his bare legs under the hospital gown.

"Gawd," he gasped, "I'm naked."

"You're fine," Burt said. "No one will see us."

"I cain't go nowhere like this," Dodo protested.

"We gotta go like this," Burt said, "because if they catch us we can say we were just looking for the bathroom."

"They got a bathroom right here in the room."

"I didn't know that." Burt said innocently. "Do you know that?" He punched Dodo in the ribs.

"No, I reckon not."

"All right then. Let's go find us a bathroom."

Burt had been in the hospital lots of times to see Betty Mae at work and once or twice for the flu. Once he'd done a little job of carpentry, building shelves in the X-ray room, and he knew that the lab was right across from the X-ray room.

He peeked out into the hall and it was empty and quiet. "Get me one of your shoes," he whispered to Dodo. Dodo went back into the room and came back with one of his brogans. Burt sneaked open the squeaky back door and motioned Dodo out onto the cement stoop and then he followed, propping the door open with Dodo's shoe so that they could get back in.

The stars were spread all to hell and gone across the early morning sky, but Burt wasn't in a poetic mood. He hurt too badly to appreciate the beauty of the night. Now on the way back he might take a look up and see them and feel like singing them a verse or two.

Gravel bit into their bare feet and Dodo did a stiff and rickety dance as they went down the walk, onto the grass, and around to the emergency entrance. Burt peeked in the glass of the door and couldn't see anyone. He opened the door ever so slowly and let Dodo go in ahead. They tiptoed past the emergency room door and up the hall, a draft coming up Burt's hospital gown to cool his privates. At the lab door he halted, his finger to his lips to quiet Dodo's harsh breathing. He looked up and down the hall, and there was no one to see. He tried the knob. The door was unlocked. He shoved Dodo in first. It was dark inside.

"We gotta have some light," he whispered, his hand searching the wall for the switch. He found it and the lights flickered on. They were in the small room used for drawing blood and the door was closed to the main part of the lab. "I think it'd be in there," he whispered. He tiptoed to the door and opened it and almost screamed. Then he regained his composure.

"Hey," he said, "we was just looking for the bathroom."

The murderer, too, had almost screamed, trapped in the lab with the door to the main room locked by key, hearing someone come into the blood drawing room, hearing the door open, standing there with five ampules of Benadryl and a hypodermic needle.

"This is convenient for both of us," the murderer said. "I was just coming down to give you an injection, and your coming here has saved me a trip. Now if you'll both just sit down in the chairs."

Both Burt and Dodo had been brought up to respect authority and there was authority in the voice, and they'd been caught in the act. They sat down meekly. The murderer injected 60 cc of epinephrine, using the holes made by the IV's which had put harmless sugar into their veins earlier.

It was very sad watching them die, holding them in the chairs as they grunted and jerked and their eyes rolled in severe pain, but it was not to be helped. They had brought it on themselves, being where they shouldn't have been. Death is always sad, but there are times when it is necessary for one's self-protection.

Chapter Ten

Four o'clock in the morning. All is quiet on the Bellamy Memorial front. Lance had made one more restless round, walking the quiet halls, conscious of the loud fall of his footsteps. Two hours before the end of the graveyard shift things started coming together in his mind, for he had made one interesting stop during the last walk around the building.

John King was lying on his back, fully clothed except for his shoes. Delphi and Lowery had said that if a man were shooting overdoses of Benadryl he'd be loggy and sleepy. King had certainly been difficult to awaken when he was needed in the emergency room.

Lance walked into the room making no attempt to be quiet. "Dr. King," he said, in a normal voice. He turned on the bedside light. Although it was August and the air conditioning system of Bellamy Memorial was far from modern, King wore a long sleeved dress shirt open at the neck. Lance picked up King's right arm by the shirt sleeve and let it drop. There was no hint of awakening. He unbuttoned the sleeve and pushed it up.

The drug problem in Clarendon was almost exclusively limited to grass and a bit of hash. Lance had seen needle marks only in training films. The arm looked normal to him. He went around to the other side of the bed and pushed the sleeve up on the left arm. There was a little mark, fresh, the type he'd seen on his own arm after having blood taken. He rebuttoned both sleeves and went into the bathroom. Under some wadded newspaper there were three caps of the sort which Delphi and Lowery said came from Benadryl. He took them, along with the piece of tissue with blood spots, and turned off the light. King had not moved.

On the way past the emergency room he stopped in. Alice Perry was sitting at the desk, head on her arms. She looked up sleepily when he cleared his throat.

"Tough night?" he asked.

"They're all tough."

"Well, it won't be long now. I can use about a half dozen eggs and a pound of bacon."

"Not me," Alice said. "I don't even want to think about anything but my bed."

"Does Dr. King stay on until the other doctors come for rounds?" Lance asked. "Or does he go off at seven, too?"

"Up until recently he had to leave here very early to be on duty at the naval hospital," Alice said. "His hours must have been changed. Like this morning he told me to leave word with the morning shift to let him sleep until he waked up."

"The naval hospital. That's up at the marine base?"

"Yes."

"Well, hang in there," Lance said.

Someone was going to have to talk with Dr. John King, and Lance thought he'd like to have Jug with him, possibly Ruben Epstein, since the hospital had a stake in it. If King were going to sleep in that would allow time. He could get some breakfast and catch an hour's sleep himself and then call Jug.

Betty Mae, the little-old-coffee-maker, served all of them one last cup. Lance made a face. Too much coffee, too little sleep. Delphi was at the desk, head down on her arms in the same position he'd seen Alice Perry in the emergency room. Lowery, seemingly tireless, was knitting. Betty Mae finished her coffee, rose, straightened her wrinkled skirt and went off down the hall. Within minutes she was back, coming at a half lope.

"Lord God above," she said, "he's gone."

"Probably just went home," Lowery said. "Woke up and decided he wanted his own bed."

"Not without his clothes," Betty Mae said.

Lance, Lowery and Betty Mae went down to room two. Burt's clothes were hanging in the closet with Dodo's. Lance discovered the shoe propping open the back door.

"Running around in a hospital gown," Betty Mae said. "That man'll be the death of me yet."

"Why would they go outside dressed in nothing but a gown?" Lowery asked.

"Lord protect us," Betty Mae said. "The medical alcohol in the lab."

Lance had to trot to keep up with her. She was a step ahead of him when they turned the corner. Delphi looked up, shooting a look of puzzlement at them as they went by the station. The lab was dark. Betty Mae threw the door open.

"Burt," she said, her voice carrying the tone of a mother scolding a naughty child. "Burt, you in there?" She flipped the light switch. The sound which came from her throat might have been made by someone gargling acid. She fell to her knees. Burt was half in, half out of the blood drawing chair. Dodo was slumped over the arm of the other chair.

"Oh, Burt, oh, God, honey, oh, Burt."

Lowery looked over Lance's shoulder and shoved past to kneel before Dodo. "Dead," she said, looking up at Lance with eyes wide.

Betty Mae stood, hand automatically brushing the back of her white uniform skirt to knock out the wrinkles. The moment of hysteria was gone.

"We'd better get Dr. King," Lowery said.

"No, not yet," Lance said quickly. "Is there a telephone in here?"

"In there," Lowery said.

Lance let the telephone ring five, six times before Jug's wife Bessie answered sleepily. He could hear her shaking Jug and calling to him. Jug had been in bed only a couple of hours. Then he was on the line. There was no easy way to tell him. Lance used as few words as possible.

"My God, boy," Jug said.

Lance's next call was to Ruben Epstein. Epstein was soon wide awake and moving. Epstein arrived first, hair unbrushed, looking like a skid row reject. "Where's Dr. King?" he asked, when he saw no one in or around the lab other than the nurses.

"We'll talk about that when Jug gets here," Lance said. "He's on his way."

"Damnit, he might have been able to do something," Epstein said.

"No," Lowery said.

Epstein bent over Burt and then Dodo, satisfying himself that they were indeed dead. "I demand to know why Dr. King wasn't called," he said, glaring at Lance.

"If you don't mind, I'd rather not discuss it now," Lance said.

Epstein growled. "All right, don't you people

have duty stations?"

The nurses, Delphi, Lowery, and Alice Perry from the emergency room, went off. Betty Mae had been standing just inside the lab, weeping quietly. Epstein put his arm over her shoulder. "Now Betty Mae, there's nothing you can do right now. Why don't you go on home. You'll be wanting to tell the kids, and after a while we'll contact you about arrangements."

Cigarette ashes falling onto his shirt, Epstein glared at Lance when they were alone. "How the hell did this happen? I thought you were here to prevent any more of this."

Lance didn't like the tone. He lowered his voice and reverted to dialect. "Boss, I'se jest a uppity black boy. I done been outclassed."

"Knock off the shit," Epstein said.

Lance heard Jug's siren coming, wailing into the emergency parking area. He met Jug at the back door. "How the hell did it happen?" Jug demanded.

"I don't know, Jug. From the look on their faces my money would be on the same way it happened to Marian Powers."

Jug was silent as they walked rapidly up the hall. He examined the scene for a moment. "What you think, boy?"

"I think we got us a doctor gone bad," Lance said.

"Now wait a goddamned minute," Epstein said.

"Hold your horses, doc," Jug said. "Why you say that, Lance?"

"Dr. King. He's been shooting up a drug called Benadryl."

"You're crazy," Epstein said.

"Now, doc, damnit, let the boy talk," Jug said.

"One of the upstairs nurses admits giving him three ampules of it. The whole stock the hospital had in the Pharmacy and at the two nurse's stations is gone. We've found caps from the ampules. The last I found were in the bathroom of the room where King's sleeping. The nurses say the stuff has a sedative effect and Dr. King is certainly sleeping. He has needle marks on his left arm."

"But why would he kill?" Jug asked. "Miss Power and then two harmless old boys like Burt and Dodo?"

"Jug, you're the sheriff, I thought I'd let you ask him that."

"Anything I hate it's a smart-assed deputy," Jug said. "All right. Tell me what else you got."

Lance made a full report. Jug listened with a thoughtful frown on his face. Lance pointed out that there had been caps from ampules in the bathroom of the room where Marian Powers had died.

"What if he thought she was asleep and shot up in the room and she saw him?" Lance asked.

"No reason to kill her," Jug rumbled.

"There's never a good reason for killing someone," Lance said, "but a lot of people die. Now I searched this hospital up and down and sideways for the container of the drug which killed Miss Powers and I didn't find it. That makes me wonder. What if it's here in the lab, maybe inside some other container. Maybe even put in a mislabeled container? What if he had a cache of stuff in here and Burt and Dodo came upon him by surprise? He'd killed once to keep his secret, not even knowing that he'd give himself away sooner or later anyhow."

"Both of them were given something in the

vein," Dr. Epstein said, having been looking over the bodies again.

"And you think they just sat still for it?" Jug asked.

"What would you do if you were in the hospital and a doctor told you you had to have an injection?" Lance asked. "Well, on second thought, you might protest, but I don't think Burt and Dodo would have."

"Makes sense," Jug said. "Well, let's have a talk with this Dr. King."

"Just a minute, Jug," Lance said.

"Now what?"

"He's asleep and judging from the way he was out he'll stay asleep for a long time. Why don't we try to find the container I've been looking for, and maybe in the process find some Benadryl if there's any left at all."

"How do you propose to do that?"

"Well, Dennis is good at things like that. I thought I'd call him and have him pick up P.J. Charlie. Then the four of us can go through this lab with P.J.'s help, testing the contents of every container if necessary."

P.J. Charlie was a little hung. He was grumbling more than a little. Dennis Watts looked as if he'd had hours to get ready to report for duty. He had even shaved. Dennis grasped the situation quickly. They closed the door on the bodies of Burt and Dodo and locked it. Then they began the search in the main portion of the lab, P.J. Charlie taking every item individually. Some were identifiable by color and smell and only a few liquids were of the same texture and clarity of an epinephrine solution. One was close. It was in a glass stoppered bottle labeled Formaldehyde.

"That ain't formaldehyde," P.J. Charlie said, sniffing the bottle.

Epstein examined the bottle and its contents. "I couldn't swear without an analysis, but my guess is that it's what you're looking for."

Dennis Watts made the other find. It was taped on the underside of the radiator toward the back. There was just room for him to get his hand under, and when he felt the taped object he loosened it carefully. The small pack contained six ampules of 50 mg Benadryl.

"Looks like you're becoming quite the detective, boy," Jug said.

"Yeah, but if I'm right, and Burt and Dodo surprised him shooting up in the lab, why no caps or tissue in the waste basket? It breaks the pattern. He left caps and tissue in other places."

"Perhaps they came in before he did it," Dennis said.

"Damnit, neither Burt nor Dodo would have thought anything about a doctor giving himself a shot," Jug said. "They're old school types. They'd think anything a doctor did was all right. To people like Burt and Dodo doctors are sort of little tin gods who can do no wrong. They must have sat down meekly in those chairs and let him give them the fatal shots." Jug pushed his hat back and wiped his forehead with his handkerchief. "For that very reason we've got to be careful, the way people and society feel about doctors. I want to do this by the book. Now we've got enough evidence, circumstantial, but enough, to collar the good doctor. Dennis, I want you to go wake up the judge and get us a warrant. Not too heavy, just enough to allow us to hold him for some questioning."

"Possession?" Dennis asked.

"This Benadryl called a narcotic, doc?" Jug asked.

"No," Epstein said.

"That won't do, then," Jug said. "Well, hell, in for a dime, in for a dollar. Make it murder. If we're wrong, we're wrong and it won't be the first time."

Dennis left and Jug turned to Lance. "While we're waiting for Dennis to get back I want you to get on the phone and see what you can find out about this Dr. King. It's so early you probably won't be able to get in touch with the chief of staff or whatever up at that naval hospital, but stay with it until you find someone who knows him, and ask some questions about how he's been performing up there and all."

It took longer than they expected. The judge had arisen early and was somewhere out beyond the mouth of the river at sunrise chasing bluefish. Dawn came and the start of a new day with the night shift going home, Lowery and Delphi walking past the waiting room where Jug and Lance sat impatiently. Delphi smiled at him and said good night.

"Pretty little gal," Jug said, when the front door closed behind them. "Were I a young buck like you—"

"And black," Lance said.

"And black," Jug said, "I'd whisper a few sweet nothings into her ears."

"You're a dirty old man," Lance grinned.

"Boy like you needs a good woman," Jug said. "No good living alone. I know you was hit and hit hard but we go on living."

"Jug, I appreciate your concern," Lance said. "But let me handle my lovelife, O.K.?"

Dennis called. Jug took it in the administrator's office. The switchboard was open and the girl on duty. Jug came back and sat down. "First things first," he said, shaking his head. "Dennis finally located the judge. He came in with a boat load of fish and refuses to leave until they're cleaned and on ice. Dennis is helping him."

"I'd like to see that," Lance said, "Dennis cleaning fish."

Lance's earlier call to the naval hospital had not been overfruitful. The doctor on emergency duty knew John King only slightly, knew that he'd been hospitalized but had had nothing to do with the case. The night supervisor of nurses gave the only hint of useful information and that was not definite. She was sure that there had been no accident, that the operation had been to remove a tumor on John King's neck.

It was past seven-thirty and it had been a long night. Lance went into the administrator's office and tried the naval hospital again. He was, after being put on hold and shuffled around, finally connected with the full colonel in charge of the naval hospital.

"They go to work early up there," Lance said, sitting down beside Jug. "I talked with the big man and he was familiar with King's case and with King. It seems that he had cancer."

"Bad?"

"The operation was a success, according to the colonel up there who did it. But it was a bad one, and then there was some therapy which can be pretty bad. King was on Demerol for a long time. The colonel denied seeing any evidence of addiction or dependence. He did admit that it was possible, because it seems that King has been on only limited duty up there for the last six weeks, since he came out of the hospital, and is currently waiting for a medical discharge. I asked the colonel why the hospital here wasn't notified and he said that the arrangements between the marine doctors who man the emergency room here on weekends was between the individual doctors and the hospital and, besides, he didn't see any reason to notify the hospital of anything, since Dr. King was a competent doctor and was fully recovered from the operation."

"He's done nothing suspicious up there?" Jug asked.

"Colonel said he was a fine doctor with a great future in civilian medicine," Lance said.

"Well, I reckon it's time for us to go talk with him about his future," Jug said, seeing Dennis coming up the front walk.

King was in the same position, on his back, sleeping soundly. It took Lance a full five minutes to shake him into a semblance of wakefulness. He leaned on one elbow and stared at them groggily.

Jug held out his hand. In the palm of it were three caps from ampules and a wad of blooded tissue.

King looked at it for long moments. "No," he said. "No, don't do that to me."

"Son, I reckon what's been done you done to yourself," Jug said. "You wanta talk about it now?"

"There's nothing to talk about," King said, sitting up, dropping his legs off the bed. "I merely was treating myself for a chronic allergic reaction."

"Now, son, you know that won't do it," Jug said. "There's more to it than that."

"I think we'll find your fingerprints on a glass

bottle down in the lab," Lance said, "one that says it's Formaldehyde but isn't."

"I don't understand," King said.

"And on a packet containing some ampules of Benadryl which was taped up under the lab radiator," Lance said.

King's reaction surprised him. "I'll be damned," he said. "So that's—" Then he closed his mouth.

"Son," Jug said, "I'm afraid we're gonna have to arrest you. You have a right to remain silent. You have a right—"

Lance listened with half his mind. He was convinced that King had been genuinely surprised to learn the location of the Benadryl. Either that or he was a good actor who could gather his wits quickly after having been awakened from a drugged sleep.

"May I ask the charge?" King said.

"Suspicion of murder," Jug said.

"The little fool," King said.

"What's that?" Jug asked.

"I'm going to die, you know," King said.

"Well, we don't have the death penalty here no more," Jug said.

"They said they got it all, but I know," King said. "I can tell. I haven't spent most of my life studying medicine for nothing. I know when I'm being conned. It's there and it's growing and I'm going to die and the damned fools wouldn't even give me something for the pain. You can't blame me for wanting to stop the pain. It's only human. I'd do it for any patient. But, no, I had to lie and steal."

"And kill." Jug said.

"No."

"Well, I'll tell you what," Jug said, "let's go

down to the office and talk about this where we can get it on paper. You want to call a lawyer?"

"Why?" King asked.

"It's your right," Dennis Watts said.

"You look fairly intelligent," King said to Dennis. "Don't you understand? I'm dead."

Dennis had his handcuffs ready. "I don't think that will be necessary," Jug said. "Will it Dr. King?"

"Please, no," King said. He slipped his feet into his shoes, wobbled when he stood. Lance took his arm and King shook off his hand.

Dennis would stay and supervise the taking of pictures and the gathering of any possible evidence in the lab. Jug didn't like to think of poor old Burt and Dodo slumped in those chairs in the lab, but they'd have to stay there until the photographer could be found and until Dennis had finished what would probably be a futile search for prints or other evidence.

The hospital had come to life. The bustle of activity seemed to be out of keeping with what they both knew was locked up down the hall in the lab. They came down the front stairs from the second floor. "Where's your car?" Jug asked. Lance told him it was out front. Jug nodded and led the way out the front door. His car was all the way at the back.

Water street was buzzing with traffic as Earlysburg came to life for another August Monday. As they neared the sidewalk, a string of heavy eighteen-wheelers, four of them, were coming into town, having unloaded ammunition at the depot on the river during the night, headed for the downtown motel favored by the long distance truckers. Lance went around and unlocked the driver's side door, then reached across to unlock the other door.

King, watching the first truck go past, said, "He's going over the speed limit."

"Oh, I don't think so," Jug said, opening the door.

"I didn't kill anyone, you know," King said.

"Well, just get in, Dr. King," Jug said.

Another truck passed with a swoosh of air and a roar of engine. King licked his lips, looked up at the sky and, timing it carefully, bolted around the front of the car. The truck driver had no opportunity to apply his brakes until the impact sent King through the air to glance off the side of Lance's car, hitting just below the window which Lance was in the process of rolling down. Then there was a hiss of heavily applied brakes and the squall of rubber as Lance was throwing open the door.

King lay crumpled twenty feet in back of the car, his feet partially under a parked vehicle. There was blood on his lips. It bubbled. He was still breathing. "Get Dr. Epstein," Lance yelled to Jug.

"Still alive, is he?" Jug asked, looking down and breathing hard from his short run.

"Not worth killing," King whispered. Lance put his ear down close.

"You're all right," he said. "You're going to be all right."

"The fool," King gasped. Blood sprinkled Lance's face and he started to draw back. King was breathing with great difficulty. "Protecting me," King whispered. "Waste. Little fool."

Someone had seen the accident from the hospital. Dr. Epstein came on the run. As he leaned down King spewed blood and heaved, legs doing an obscene little dance. Then there was nothing to do but carry him, face covered, to the emergency room to await the arrival of Bridge Truval's hearse.

Lance stood in the hall, moodily smoking, his mouth raw from coffee and cigarettes, his eyes scratchy. Jug came out and joined him.

"I heard part of it," Jug said.

"Jug, I don't think he's the killer."

Jug pushed back his hat and sighed. "I'm damned sorry to hear you say that."

Dennis Watts came down the hall. "I just heard," he said. "I guess that closes the file."

"Lance don't think so," Jug said. "The doctor said some things before he died. Seems like we now got to do what there's a famous French phrase for which I never can remember." Dennis looked at him questioningly. "What the man said when he was dying seemed to indicate that there's a lady involved. He said something about someone protecting him. Called that person a little fool. Seems to me that's a phrase a man would use to describe a woman."

"Which woman?" Dennis asked.

"Mrs. Carpenter, I'm afraid," Lance said. "She admitted to me that she had given him Benadryl. When he told him about the stuff you found under the radiator he looked surprised and I think he was going to say, 'So that's where she hid it.'"

"Lance, you get very little to go on," Jug said.

"Nothing solid," Lance admitted, "but she'd been through an emotional crisis lately. I think we put pressure on her she'll break right easy."

"It'd be easier just to close it," Jug said. "Say that King's suicide was an admission of guilt." He held up his hand when Lance started to speak. "Oh, I know. I wouldn't sleep easy either. I might have to come to this hospital a lot sooner than you, boy. And I'd hate to think there was someone running around here in uniform that would watch three people die." He sighed again. "How you wanta work it?"

"Me and you, if you don't mind," Lance said.

"And good old Dennis stays to clean up the mess," Dennis said. His grin told them he didn't really mind.

"Well, Dennis, that's the way the fishtail flips," Jug said. "All right boy. It's your show. I'll just follow your lead, you having talked to her before."

"No time better than right now," Lance said. "While she's still tired from a night's work, a little sleepy, maybe a little saddened by her lover's death."

Jug didn't believe in unnecessary walking. They went out the back door to Jug's car. Outside of town on what had once been a blueberry farm, treeless, low, damp in rainy weather to the point of overflowing septic tanks, there was a development of low-cost housing financed by the Farmers Home Administration. The lower the income of the resident the more interest was paid on his behalf by the government. Lately blacks had been moving in and, as a result, there were several empty houses. Tolerance had not yet come to Blueberry Acres. Lorna and Don Carpenter lived in a house with red shutters at the end of one of the curved streets. Behind the house were slash pine woods, cut over by the pulpwood companies and left in tangled, dead disarray. There were two cars and a motorcycle in the driveway. A small dog, a cross between mutt and mongrel, barked a greeting and then came forward wagging his tail.

The doorbell was answered by Don Carpenter. He was unshaven, dressed in a white cotton tee shirt and faded jeans. His eyes narrowed when he saw the two uniformed men. Jug said, "Mornin', Don."

"Jug, what can I do for you?" Carpenter asked, his voice not as firm as he would have liked.

"Well, actually," Jug said, "we've come to see Lorna. She's home from work, is she?"

"Yeah, sure," Carpenter said. "She's in the shower. Why you wanta see her?"

"Just about something happened at the hospital," Jug said. "You wanta go tell her we're here?"

"Sure," Carpenter said. "Coffee on the stove you want some. Cups on the counter."

Lance and Jug stood in the living room, a small room carpeted in green, with white walls and Sears furniture. The smell of old grease came from the kitchen through an archway at the end of the room. They could hear the sound of the shower running down the hall to the left. They heard Don Carpenter open the bathroom door and say, "Lorna, the sheriff is here and wants to see you." They did not hear her answer. After what seemed to be hours, but was actually only five minutes or so, the shower stopped. Carpenter came back and went into the kitchen. He came out with a cup of coffee.

"Sure you won't have some?" he asked.

Both shook their heads.

"This about those pranks been going on?" Carpenter asked.

"In general," Lance said.

"Don," Jug said, "you got something you have to do, you go right ahead."

"No," he said, laughing. "I happen to be at

136

leisure right now."

"Well," Jug said, "if you don't mind, we'd like to talk to Lorna alone."

"I don't know, Jug," Carpenter said. "She's pretty high-strung, and if you're going to talk about that stuff at the hospital I might need to be here. She gets pretty excited."

"We won't excite her any more than we have to," Jug said. "Why don't you go take a ride on that motorcycle or something."

"I think I'll stay," Carpenter said.

Jug shrugged. He looked at the prints of old motorcars on the wall. They heard the bathroom door open and close and then, a few minutes later, she came out wrapped in a terrycloth bathrobe, covered from chin to ankles, feet bare, hair damp from the shower.

"Miz Carpenter," Jug said in greeting.

"Why do you want to see me?" she asked, her voice calm but cool.

"I'm afraid we have some bad news for you," Lance said, taking over. "You wanna sit down?"

"No," she said simply.

"Well, just after you left work Dr. John King was killed," Lance said, keyed to watch her reaction.

"How terrible," she said, in that calm, cool voice. "How did it happen?"

"What makes that bad news for you?" Carpenter asked her.

"Don, you wanta just listen?" Jug asked.

"No, damnit, I don't want to just listen," Carpenter flared. "What the hell do you think this is?" He turned to Lorna. "So there was something going on between you and that Marine prick."

"Take it easy," Jug said.

"I want to thank you very much," Lorna said bitterly, looking at Lance.

"I wanta know what you know about her and that marine bastard," Carpenter yelled at them.

"And I want you to sit down and shut up," Jug said, "before I get mad. I didn't come here to cause no domestic quarrel. I came to ask Lorna a few questions and by God we're gonna do it if we have to gag you, Don."

Carpenter turned away angrily and lit a cigarette. Lorna had taken a seat on the couch, erect on the forward edge, her hands in her lap, the robe showing a length of leg below the knee. "There was nothing between me and Dr. King," she said wearily. "I told you that, Lance. I told you that my relationship to him was purely professional. I told you that I once gave him three ampules of Benadryl because he told me he needed it for a friend."

"You didn't tell me you went out with him," Lance said.

"Sonofabitch," Carpenter shouted, moving toward Lorna. Jug interposed himself.

"I ain't gonna warn you again," he said.

"Of course I didn't go out with him," Lorna said.

"Lorna, I have a witness who will say you did," Lance said. "She was with you."

"Oh, that," she said.

"That," Lance said. "You wanta tell us about it?"

"That was way last year. In the winter. That was while I was on the three-to-eleven shift. It was quiet at the hospital when Pond and I got off duty—"

"Pond?" Jug asked.

"Delphi Pond," Lance said.

"Oh, the pretty little girl downstairs," Jug said.

"Pond and I were going down to the tavern. Don was out of town and I wasn't ready to come home to an empty house."

"How damned convenient," Carpenter said. Jug glared at him.

"We were getting ready to go out and Dr. King came up and said something about needing some air and asked us if we minded if he went with us for a cup of nonhospital coffee. Since I had to come back by the hospital to get home I took Dr. King with me in my car and Delphi drove her own. We met at the tavern and Del and I had a beer and Dr. King drank coffee. That's all there was to it."

"Then Delphi left you with him," Lance said.

"Yes, but we stayed only five minutes or so after she left, then I dropped him off at the hospital and came on home."

"Mrs. Carpenter," Lance said, "did you wipe your fingerprints off the container in the lab?"

"I don't understand," she said, shaking her head.

"You wiped them off the breakfast trays."

"No, I didn't. I mean, if you're talking about the incident upstairs, I had no occasion or reason to touch either tray. I was off duty and went immediately home that morning."

Lance was worried. She was so deadly calm. No hint of the agitation she'd shown when she told him about her attempted suicide. He decided on one more shot. "Was it epinephrine you gave Burt and Dodo?"

"Let's get back to that Marine bastard," Don Carpenter said. "How many more times did you go have a beer with him?"

"Boy," Jug said. "Your wife is being questioned

as a possible suspect in a murder case. Cain't you think of nothing but yourself?"

"Murder?" Carpenter said. "You're crazy."

"Was it epinephrine?" Lance asked. "How did you get them to let you shoot it into them?"

Lorna shook her head sadly. "No," she said, "you know I didn't. I couldn't. No reason."

"You were in love with King and protecting him. He told me that as he was dying. You killed Marian Powers because she saw King shooting up in her room. You killed Burt and Dodo because they walked in on you in the lab when you were getting Benadryl from under the radiator where you'd hidden it."

"I once tried to kill myself," Lorna said quietly.

"What?" Don exploded.

She looked up at him and smiled. "Yes," she said. "I disliked myself that much, Don. What I didn't realize at the time was that it was you I hated, and not myself."

"Hey," Don said.

"I didn't sleep with John King," she said. "I have never so much as held his hand. If, in the future, I see a man I'd like to sleep with, I'm going to. Because I want you out, Don. I'd like for you to go now. I don't need you anymore."

"Hey," Don said, "where the hell would I go?"

"That's your problem," Lorna said, rising. "And now I'd like you all go to, please. I'm tired. I have had a long night and I have another one facing me tonight. If you have any other questions I'll be glad to answer them, but I'm afraid I can't help you. I have killed no one. I even failed when I tried to kill myself."

"Yeah, you guys better go," Carpenter said. "I told you you'd upset her."

"Sheriff, could you please see to it that he leaves?" Lorna asked.

"Well, Miz Carpenter, there's ways to do that," Jug said.

"Goddamn, that's the way you feel, I'll go," Don said, heading for the bedrooms.

"You satisfied, boy?" Jug asked Lance.

"You got any questions?" Lance asked, feeling rather helpless.

"I don't think this little lady would kill a fly," Jug said.

"Thank you," Lorna said. "I wish I could help. In spite of what you might think, I'm proud of my profession. That's the one thing that pulled me through when I was—when—"

"I think I understand," Jug said. "Now personally, Miz Carpenter, I believe you when you say you had nothing to do with those killings. That don't mean we might not have to talk to you again."

"I won't mind," she said.

"You think about it. Think about anything you might have seen or heard that might give us some place to go," Jug said. "We got three people dead at the hospital shouldn't be dead, and they were all friends of mine."

"I agree with you in thinking that Dr. King didn't kill them," Lorna said. "He was an excellent doctor, a kind man. I've seen him labor over a man who was obviously dead, trying and trying to get his heart going again. By the way, you never did say how he was killed."

Jug told her. He strung the story out, and Lance began to realize that he was waiting for Don Carpenter to leave. When Carpenter came out of the bedrooms he was carrying a bag.

"I'll send for the rest of my stuff," he said.

"Goodbye, Don," Lorna said calmly.

Carpenter slammed out the door. Jug's car was behind him. He drove across the lawn, leaving deep tread marks in the sandy soil.

"One more question," Lance said. "You began to suspect that Dr. King was shooting up the Benadryl, didn't you?"

"I suspected, but I didn't know."

"You ever mention your suspicions to anyone, talk about him with anyone?"

"No, not really. Everyone speculated on what was wrong with him, the operation. He just said it was an accident. We used to talk about what a handsome man he was."

"We?" Lance asked.

"Oh, everyone. All the nurses. Del thought he was handsome. Lowery. Alice Perry in the emergency room actually drooled over him."

"Anything between King and Alice?"

"Alice is black and has five kids," Jug said.

"It's a new world out there, Sheriff Honk," Lance said. "Sometimes, even in the south, it's black and white together, baby."

"No," Lorna said. "I don't think so."

"Anyone at all? Did he go out with anyone? Seem to be interested in anyone particular?" Lance asked.

"No, really. He was always very businesslike when he was at the hospital."

"All right, Miz Carpenter. We know you're tired," Jug said. "We won't bother you no more."

In the car Jug started the air conditioner. It belched a rubbery smell. He grumbled, turned it off and rolled down the window. "Might trade cars with you for a few days," he said.

"I'll report you to the Civil Rights Commission," Lance answered.

"Yeah, well that's all the gratitude I get," Jug said. "Whole county after my ass, three unsolved murders, and my deputy won't even take pity on an old man who's sweating his balls off."

Lance chuckled. Dogs followed the car, barking. Kids were coming out to yelp and run on the scraggly lawns. They rode in silence until they were off the development streets and onto the highway.

"Well, what do you think, boy?" Jug asked.

"I think she sold me," Lance said. "And where does that leave us?"

"It leaves us facing a primary, with the hospital a big issue and what's happened there makes it worse. You'll have to excuse me talking politics with Burt and Dodo dead back there, but if I lose the election then we'd never have a chance to do anything about it, would be?"

"You won't lose," Lance said.

"Won't I? I took the town drunk a couple of half-gallons of moonshine so's he could have a party after locking me out of my own jail, and then when I got him out I put him in the hospital and got him killed. And the whole county's tore up over this hospital issue and they're going to vote hospital instead of me, and you're going to be out of a job, boy."

"Maybe we ought to call on the SBI for a little help."

"City slickers?" Jug grunted. "We got one advantage over them, boy. Even with all their training and high powered equipment. We know the people. We know that someone, some woman, is running around loose after three murders, that is if we're going to accept the word of a dying man that he didn't do them, and I think I do. We know she knows something about medicine and probably works at the hospital. That narrows it down a damned lot. We got Mrs. Carpenter, Mrs. Lowery, Alice Perry, and Delphi Pond."

Lance looked at him quickly when Delphi's name was mentioned. Jug did not miss the look. "Hadn't even thought of her in that connection, huh?" Jug asked. "Well, look at it this way. If she was protecting King, the killer, it meant she was in love with him and maybe had something going with him. That pretty well eliminates a few of the women on the late shift, don't it? I mean, I can't quite see Betty Mae Scoggins having an affair with King and then killing old Burt. She loved that no good sonofabitch. And there's Mrs. Maddock, the aide upstairs with Miz Carpenter, old, old as I am, and fat. It's far-fetched to think about Alice Perry like that, too, with her five kids and all, even if she is still a youngish woman. And Lowery? Hell, that woman has been the rock of Bellamy Hospital for so long that I don't think she'd do anything to hurt the hospital. Other hand, her husband's been dead some five years now and she's not ancient, is she? Little older than King was, but not too old."

"I can't see it being Lowery," Lance said.

"And who does that leave?"

"Mrs. Carpenter and Delphi," Lance said.

"And you said you believed Carpenter," Jug said quietly.

"And that leaves us with nobody, because I know damned well it wasn't Del."

"Ah," Jug said. "So it begins, huh?"

"You and the horse you rode in on," Lance said.

But in his bed, in the brief few moments before

he lost it all in sleep, he thought about Del and when he thought of her in bed with Dr. King he couldn't believe it and when he thought of her shooting deadly stuff into three people he couldn't believe that. And the most amazing thing about it was that he could think of Del without having the mutilated body of Glenda floating up from hell to blot out Del's face. For the first time in almost a year he was able to think about Glenda without all those waves of guilt. The world is a helluva nice place, but it can be mean and when it's mean you fight and you don't always win. He himself had almost been killed trying to save Glenda and it wasn't his fault. It was almost as if the madman who killed her was a natural force, like a hurricane or an earthquake. You try to stand up to things like that and sometimes you're too small.

And love dies. Love had died in Lorna Carpenter and she realized it, perhaps rather suddenly, and she'd sent Don Carpenter packing. Love had died in Glenda and she'd gone packing off to her mother and then into the bed of old Laconius Iboe, the intellectual wonder, and it was sheer accident that she'd been around at the wrong time, because Jack Boydston was coming for Lance, not Glenda, and she'd been caught in the teeth of the hurricane and chewed up.

Not that he was in love with Delphi. No, not yet. Maybe not ever. But he could picture her face and her slightly slanted eyes and the fullness of her mouth and the texture of her brown skin. In the face of death he was seeing a glimmer of life.

It was impossible to think of Delphi as being King's woman and of killing three people for him.

Chapter Eleven

It was just as impossible as before. Tuesday morning. Hot before nine o'clock. Sticky. Toast and cereal for breakfast. Dennis and Jug already in the office making remarks about deputies keeping banker's hours. Reports to write. Jug glum about the newspapers' stories about the latest murders, the implied incompetence of all involved, law officers and the hospital.

While Jug fumed over the papers, the chief deputy motioned Lance into the inner office. "While you were sleeping I took care of the details," Dennis said.

"You're a good man," Lance said. "A good white man, true, but still a good man."

"Seems your boy King was loaded," Dennis said.

"Yeah?"

"I contacted his family in Philadelphia. Old rich, I gather. Stiff upper lip and all. No shock when they were notified. I talked with his mother. She took it like a brick. She said, 'Oh, isn't that terrible, poor, poor boy. And just having suffered through that terrible operation.' "

" 'Poor, poor boy,' " Lance said, remembering the sound of King's body smashing against the door of his car to leave a large indentation.

"I got curious and contacted the Philadelphia

police. Sure enough the King family is well known there. Quite rich. John King, himself, came into something like three or four million when he was thirty."

"Fuzz up there tell you anything about him might be useful?"

"He was a sterling character. No faults. Top five percent of his class, Yale School of Medicine. I got his service record, too. Fine officer. No demerits from anyone who ever knew him, it seems. Almost too good to be true."

"So he ends up shooting junk and running into a truck," Lance said, "while worrying about having terminal cancer."

"Yeah, well, money isn't everything, is it?" Dennis asked.

"Dennis, somewhere there's got to be a handle we can grab," Lance said, "I wonder if I could have a day to run up to Jax and talk to people who worked with King."

"I don't see why not. It's quiet. The old man's going to be involved in campaigning. When do you want to go?"

"Right now," Lance said.

"Adios," Dennis said. "But don't forget those reports first thing when you get back."

It was a fine day for driving with the air conditioner on. Traffic was light to Wilmington and then thinned out again on the other side. He reached the sprawling Marine base just before noon and followed the directions of the marine at the gate to the hospital. The hospital was late federal in style, huge and brick and grim. Well kept grounds. People in wheelchairs in the shade of the live oaks, and inside the usual hospital smell and pastel walls and nurses in uniform.

Lance had to wait several minutes to see Colonel Elvin Wheeler. He explained his mission. Wheeler himself had not been on a close personal basis with Dr. King. He was shocked by King's death, but the boy was having problems and wouldn't take his advice and see a psychiatrist. Thought the cancer was terminal when Wheeler would have bet hat and ass that they'd gotten it all and that King would have had no further problems.

Lance left Wheeler's office with the name of the man who Wheeler thought had been closest to King, a Dr. James Voit. Dr. Voit was in the operating room and would be there for at least two more hours. Lance found the hospital cafeteria and had a good slice of meatloaf, red beans and collards. The cafeteria was crowded and he had to wait for a table. The contrast between the naval hospital and the Bellamy Memorial was astounding. The naval hospital reminded Lance of a huge and complicated factory run by impersonal people. He was amazed that the security there was not much better than at Bellamy. People seemed to be able to go where they wanted. There were a lot of uniforms, of course, but a man in a uniform could walk in and steal the operating room as far as Lance could see. He wondered when the terrorists of the big cities were going to latch on to the fact that most hospitals are as open as department stores. Talk about a real panic, how about a group of nuts taking over a large hospital and holding critically ill patients hostage for ten billion dollars or so.

With people waiting, he couldn't linger over his meal. He found himself back on the third floor waiting with only two-month-old copies of *Time* magazine to read. He had found an interesting article on murder in Detroit, murder city, when a tall man in surgical green came into the small waiting area, facemask down around his neck, green hat covering his hair.

"I'm Dr. Voit. You wanted to see me?"

Lance did not show his surprise. Dr. James Voit was pure Africa, looking as if his blood were undiluted by anything other than pure black. He was lean and had long, graceful fingers.

"Dr. Voit, I suppose you've heard about the death of Dr. John King," Lance said.

"Yes." There was a change in Voit's eyes. "Yes, goddamn it, I heard."

A woman and three teenagers came into the waiting room. The teenagers started grabbing for magazines. "Is there somewhere we can talk?" Lance asked.

"My office."

Voit led the way down the hall and sank into a chair behind a desk in a tiny cubicle of a room with gray walls. "Now, just what is there to talk about?" he asked, looking at his watch.

"Colonel Wheeler said that you probably knew Dr. King better than anyone," Lance said. "We have a few unanswered questions—"

"John would have nothing to do with murder," Voit said.

"Hey, brother," Lance said, "we don't think so either, but we do think that someone who knew him well might have killed to protect him, to keep anyone from finding out he was hooked."

"Is that public knowledge?" Voit asked. "John King was too much man to have his name disgraced."

"We're keeping it pretty tight at the moment," Lance said. "You knew, then?"

"We're busy around here, as you can see. I'm afraid that I was so involved in my work that I wasn't paying enough attention to John. I caught him just last week and he admitted that he was having some trouble. We were going to work on it when he came back here yesterday."

"And knowing that he was on drugs you let him come down to our little hospital to practice medicine."

Voit darkened. "Even on drugs John was one helluva doctor."

"Well, that's not the point anymore, is it?" Lance asked. "The point is that we've got three bodies down there in Clarendon. King could have told us who he was involved with, but he made an appointment with an eighteen-wheeler before he would do it. Do you have any idea? Ever hear him mention any names? A woman?"

"He said there were some surprisingly good nurses at Bellamy," Voit said. "He mentioned the emergency room nurse as being first class, but I've forgotten her name."

"Alice Perry?"

"A black woman."

"Yes. What did he say about Alice?"

"Only that she was a crackerjack, good as any emergency room nurse he'd ever worked with."

"What about Lorna Carpenter? Ever hear him mention her?"

"No, I don't think so."

"A Mrs. Lowery?"

"The iron woman of the night shift," Voit said.

"He was quite impressed with her, too."

"Any hint of personal involvement?"

"None that he mentioned."

"Delphi Pond?"

"A cute, young, black chick?"

"Yes."

"He said I should go down with him, that there was a real beauty working the late watch. I think that was her name."

"Would King have backed off from a personal relationship with a black?" Lance asked.

"Of course not," Voit said. "I was his best friend. More than that, I owed him."

"Wanta tell me about that?"

"We were in premed together. I was having one hell of a rough time financially. John went into his own pocket and made me a loan. I haven't paid it back yet, but I will. I came into the Marines just after taking my specialty. John was already in, and he said the conditions here were great for working and learning."

"So in effect King paid your way through med school?"

"A loan."

"Has he helped other people?"

"Yes, one or two. He was a dedicated man and he liked helping others. He believed in his work. That's why it was so bad when they found cancer and it hit him hard, and, I guess, scared hell out of him. He was rich, young, handsome. He was a brilliant doctor. And to have that happen to him was something he couldn't believe. I'm sure he went to his death believing that he was terminal in spite of all we could do to convince him."

"Did you do the surgery?"

"No, Colonel Wheeler was chief surgeon. I assisted." Voit looked at his watch again. "Look, is this really helping in any way?"

"How about women in his life?" Lance asked.

"He had no time for them."

"Everyone has time for women," Lance said. "None?"

"In school he'd date girls for important functions."

"How about you, Dr. Voit? How about the women in your life?"

"I don't like that question, but I'm married and have a fourteen-month-old son."

"You wouldn't describe King as a ladies' man, then?"

"He lived for his work."

"He was having an affair with someone at Bellamy. In his dying breath he called her a little fool for protecting him."

Voit looked thoughtful and reached for a cigarette, patting a pocketless smock. Lance offered one of his and lit it.

"I think I struck a nerve there," Lance said, in his Amos voice.

Voit shook his head. "Look, he's dead. Can't we leave him alone?"

"A nice old lady and two men are dead, too," Lance said. "The two men were old and sort of useless, but they weren't ready to have an overdose of epinephrine pumped into them."

"Oh, goddamn," Voit said, standing to look out the small window behind his desk.

"Dr. Voit," Lance said softly.

"Will you promise me one thing?" Voit said, turning to look down at Lance. "Will you promise me that you'll do everything possible to keep it out of the papers?"

"If possible. As you say, he's dead. I wouldn't enjoy heaping dirt on top of the dirt they're going to throw in his face."

"The little fool he mentioned. You're looking in the, uh, the wrong direction."

"Are you saying what I think you're saying?" Lance asked.

"He didn't know I knew. He never made a move toward me. I had Caren. I was in love. He was my friend in spite of it. I'd say, brother, that you should look for a bright young man with an interest in medicine."

But Lance couldn't think of any bright young men with an interest in medicine around Bellamy Memorial Hospital. Young men were scarce. There was P.J. Charlie in the lab and the orderlies, Jimbo, Deother, and Billy Smith on the afternoon shift.

"Dr. Voit, I appreciate this. It at least gives us a few new ideas."

"I hope you find the killer."

"We'll find him."

He thought it over on the way home. P.J. Charlie was out. P.J. liked girls. P.J. was a loving fool and Lance knew that from old times. What did he know about the others? The three orderlies had one thing—two things—in common. They were young and they were black. An orderly's job was not the best in the world and men didn't usually make a career of it. They came and went at Bellamy, usually local teenagers or slightly older boys who worked at the job for a year or so and moved on to something more promising. Jimbo had been there longer than any of them and he was the oldest. Billy Smith was just out of high school. Deother Robinson was, probably, in his early twenties, twenty-two at most. No, probably younger. Just a year out of high school, working at Bellamy.

Deother would have had the opportunity. Was he the one with the motive? He worked the midnight shift. He was often out of sight, sleeping in an empty room when he was not needed. All of the incidents and all of the murders had taken place when Deother was on shift or shortly before his going on or coming off shift.

Lance tried to picture Deother in his mind. A strong, well-built, handsome boy, thin and graceful. Intelligent eyes. Well-kept short hair. Lance didn't know him that well, had never spent any time with him. He remembered Deother as a teeny-bopper, playing basketball for the high school. But he had not been observant enough at that time to remember whether or not he'd ever seen Deother with girls. Back in those days Lance himself was looking harder at the girls than he was at male teenagers.

It was early evening when he turned onto the Earlysburg road, the sun red in the west behind him as he entered town. He went to the office. The night man was already on duty. Jug was off out in the county at a fishfry looking for votes. He called Dennis Watts and got no answer. The duty man said Dennis was probably flying. Lance drove to the airport and Dennis' plane was just coming in for one of those perfect landings in which Dennis prided himself. Lance watched as the Bonanza came up the runway, slowed, turned toward the pumps and the office, and then wheeled expertly to the left into the open hangar. Dennis got out and waved at him and then went through his after-flight check while tying down the aircraft. Lance walked over.

"Anything interesting?" Dennis asked, finishing and standing up after making the last tie down.

Lance told him. Dennis whistled. "Dynamite."

"I promised a brother I'd try to keep Dr. King's sexual preferences quiet," Lance said. "I don't see any reason, unless it's necessary to the case, to break it, do you?"

"The less said about it the better," Dennis said. "Think of what the hospital opponents could do with that one. Not only a nest of murderers but a nest of perverts, too." Dennis rubbed his chin. "Do we pick him up?"

Lance shook his head. "What have we got?"

"You're right. Not much."

"I want to spend one more night at the hospital," Lance said.

"Yes, I guess so. I'll contact Jug when he gets home, but it'll be late I'd guess. I'll be standing by at home if you need me. Remember that he's killed three people."

"Won't I though," Lance said grimly.

Chapter Twelve

Lance enjoyed one of the world's best hamburgers at The Spot, juke-beer-hamburger-hangout, a weathered old false-fronted store in what was still called, by many, Jabbertown, the black section of Earlysburg. Balls Gore, proprietor, Carolina basketball fan still reliving the glories of his team almost making it during the past season, big, black and friendly, put extra relish on it and, after filling an order for a group of teen-agers in the back, leaned on the counter to talk with Lance.

Lance listened to Balls brag about Dean Smith's success in recruiting for the next basketball season, nodded with satisfaction at the statistics of a tall black boy from the New York area, finished his hamburger and sipped draft beer. P.J. Charlie came in while Lance was on his second beer and Balls was just getting wound up in a rehash of the Marquette game. P.J. Charlie had his plastic pint, the portable Purple Jesus container, in his pocket. Lance declined and Balls accepted, sloshing a few ounces into a beer glass.

"I dunno why we all stay on in such a poor town," P.J. Charlie said. Lance grinned, knowing what was coming. It was P.J. Charlie's favorite joke. "This town is so poor it can't afford a town drunk, and now that ole Burt's dead we all gonna have to take turns."

Lance groaned dutifully. Balls told one about a

brother, a Jew, and an Irishman. Lance was in no hurry. When the time was right he asked, "Seen Deother Robinson in here today?"

"He don't come around much," Balls said. "Studying, he says."

"For what?" Lance asked.

"Say he goin' off to college soon," Balls said.

Sometimes it's like that. It falls into place. Lance said, "How he gonna do that? His family poor as dirt." It was becoming a habit with him, falling into the pattern of Jabbertown speech, coming out of it when he was out of the quarter.

"He talkin' some jive 'bout a scholarship," P.J. Charlie said.

"What he say?"

"Say he's off to college come the fall," P.J. said.

"Say where this scholarship come from?"

"Deother, he don't talk much," P.J. said.

"He goin' 'round with anyone in particular these days?" Lance asked.

P.J. Charlie shrugged. Balls said, "He usually alone he comes in here."

"Either one of yawl ever hear anyone say anything might lead you to think ole Deother kind of funny?" Lance asked.

"Naw," P.J. Charlie said. "I seen him with foxes."

"That don't mean he ain't no switch-hitter," Balls said, intrigued by the hint of gossip.

"Well, I ain't accusin'," Lance said. "Yawl say I said it, I call you liars."

'Where there's smoke," Balls said.

"Balls, you just forget I said anything, hear?"

"Right on," Balls said. "I done forgot."

"Why you asking about ole Deother?" P.J. wanted to know when Balls went off to fill an order for a couple of young people who had just come in.

"Just askin'," Lance said. "See you, P.J. I'm splitting."

"Wanta go ride and have a few?"

"Not tonight," Lance said. He left the right money on the counter. He drove slowly through his town. Bugs hit the windshield and flew off at the slow speed. A dog barked as he turned onto P.J. Charlie's street and parked in front of the garage apartment. A mosquito hit him on the neck as he walked across the lawn. Next door the lights were on in John Hawkins' living room and there was the sound of a TV. He knocked.

Hawkins was recently retired as superintendent of the once all black high school in Jabbertown. When he recognized Lance he said, "Come in, boy." He turned the sound down on the TV and invited Lance to sit.

"I won't keep you from your program long, Mr. Hawkins. I just wondered if you remember a student named Deother Robinson."

"Deother? Of course." Hawkins had just a hint of southern accent. "Nice lad. Worked hard but didn't have it up here." He tapped his forehead. "Study as he might he just could not stay on the honor roll. Made it when he was a sophomore, if I remember correctly, and then, try as he might, he could not make it again."

"Did he ever mention his ambitions to you?" Lance asked.

"As a matter of fact, he did. He wanted to go into medicine." Hawkins sighed. "I tried to explain to him that medicine was an extremely competitive field and that only the very top students could get into a medical school. I think, perhaps, I was instrumental in interesting him in his work at the hospital. I told him there were fields allied to medicine which could be most rewarding."

"You haven't by any chance talked with Deother lately?" Lance asked.

"Strangely enough, yes," Mr. Hawkins said. "Just, oh, two to three days ago, as a matter of fact. He told me that he had arranged to enter a university. I questioned him, being interested in how he managed it, but he was rather coy about it. He smiled and said that never mind how, he was going and that he'd show all of us how wrong we had been about him."

"Do you think it possible that he could have lined up some sort of grant or scholarship?"

"It's possible. This day and time even the average student—" He laughed. "If he's black, that is, can get a grant or a scholarship."

"But you don't know of any? Haven't heard of any in connection with Deother?"

"If he got a scholarship it was not through the usual machinery of Clarendon County's schools. I still maintain my contacts and I'm sure that someone would have mentioned such an unusual occurence."

"You've been a great help, Mr. Hawkins," Lance said, standing.

"Is Deother in some sort of trouble?"

"Like they say on the TV," Lance drawled in his comic voice, "this is just routine, Mr. Hawkins."

Hawkins limped to the door to let Lance out. Once, during the time of troubles, he'd been hit on the foot by a whole brick during a school fracas. The toes had not healed straight. "I've never had a chance to tell you, Lance, that we're proud of you."

"Thank you," Lance said.

"Yes, proud," Hawkins said. He grinned. "Especially considering your rather shaky beginnings."

"Left handed compliments are better than none," Lance grinned back. "Goodnight, sir."

Time to kill. Nancy Wilson on his changer, speakers turned up loud enough to risk a few yells from Miss Annie Mae Duncan, next door. The clock frozen. A feeling of urgency. He forced himself to wait until the dot of eleven before leaving, still in uniform, .38 in place on his belt, hat pulled down low over his eyes. The graveyard shift was just getting underway at the hospital. There was no one at the first-floor nurse's station. He sat down and waited. Lowery came up the hall from the patient wing.

"I'm glad to see you," Lowery said. "I'm beginning to feel as if we need a bodyguard around this place."

"Anything else happen?" Lance asked, concerned.

"We don't need anything else happening, my God," Lowery said. "Is this a business or a social call?" Delphi had rounded the corner of the hall, walking straight and proud, tray in hand. Lowery smiled as she watched Lance's face.

"Business and social," Lance said. "I've fallen madly in love with you and want to take you away from all this."

"Old silver tongue," Lowery said, going behind the desk.

Delphi was smiling. "Hi," she said brightly. He felt a prickle of pleasure as he smiled back. "Keeping us company again tonight?"

"Not all night, I hope," Lance said.

"Oh? Too bad. We've grown accustomed to your face."

"I think that could be set to music," Lance said.

"Well, back to the grind," Delphi said. "With Betty Mae out, it's keeping us hopping. That white woman in room seven uses the bedpan every five minutes."

While they were both behind the desk, Lance got up and leaned over the desk. "There's a possibility of some excitement around here tonight. I don't think it'll be anything serious, but if something starts, make yourself scarce and keep out of the way."

Lowery looked at him questioningly. "You know who, then?"

"I think so," Lance said. "But don't ask now. Just keep your eyes open, O.K.?"

"If I hear a noise I'll climb under the desk," Delphi said.

"That's what I mean," Lance said. Delphi looked back at him once she went down the hall toward the patient's rooms.

"Lance, she's quite a girl," Lowery said.

"Playing cupid, Mrs. Lowery?"

"Well," she grinned. "Why not?"

But Lance had other things on his mind. He walked down the patients' wing, checking rooms. He winked at Delphi as she came out of room seven.

Upstairs, Lorna Carpenter nodded hello. Lance went past her desk, pushed open the swinging door to the operating room, found it empty. He came back and went down the hall toward the rear steps. Deother came out of a room toward the back with a bedpan in his hands. Lance said, "What's happening, brother."

"Same old shit," Deother said, grinning down at his burden. He pushed open the door to the hall bath with his shoulder. Lance followed him in. Deother turned and looked at him curiously.

"Been meaning to have a chat with you," Lance said. "Hear you're going off to college?"

Deother put the bedpan on top of the waste basket and reached for a cigarette before asking, "Where you hear that?"

"Oh, around."

"Don't believe everything you hear," Deother said.

"You not going to college?"

"You see me getting into a college? See me with the money to go to college?" He was looking at Lance over his hands as he used a butane lighter to fire up.

"Always a possibility of a grant or a scholarship," Lance said. He was leaning back against the wall, trying to pretend to be at ease. He didn't want Deother to suspect that he was about to be hit with a little zinger or two.

"Sheeit," Deother said, blowing smoke. "Well, was one possibility, but it fell through."

Lance felt the way he felt just before a big cobia, teased out from the shadow of a buoy, finally got up his nerve to take the dangling wad of squid which hid a very sharp hook.

"King loused you up by running into the front of a truck, huh?" Lance asked, his voice low and calm.

There was only a slight reaction, a tightening of the lips around the cigarette, a long drag. "I don't know what you're jiving," Doether said. He dropped the cigarette into the bedpan and picked it up. "Well, here's to it," he said, whipping the bedpan up and sloshing the contents directly into Lance's face. The smell assaulted him and paralyzed him momentarily, giving Deother time to land a carefully aimed haymaker on the left point of his chin. Lance went down as if he'd been hit by a truck himself, not even feeling the hardness of the tile floor, no longer smelling the vile odors.

Far in the distance he heard a door slam. Stars flashed in his brain and faded as he was pushing himself up. His eyes stung. He ripped paper towels from the holder and, running, swabbed his face. There was the sound of running footsteps going down the front stairs.

He was still seeing spots before his eyes as he started to run. He went full tilt into Mrs. Maddock, the matronly aide, coming out of a room. She bounced off the wall and caught herself before she went all the way to the floor, Lance sprawling full length, feet digging as he came back up. He took the down stairs three at a time and slid into the first-floor hallway. There was a white form sprawled in front of the nurse's station. He ran and knelt. Lowery was looking up at him crosseyed, actually crosseyed. He patted her cheeks.

"I'm all right," she said. "What the hell?"

"Which way did he go?"

Her eyes widened as she remembered. "He's got Delphi."

It hit him like a brick, Glenda walking in just as Jack Boydston had overpowered him, Glenda lying on the table up there in the shack in the marsh, belly opened up. And now Delphi. "Where?" he asked harshly.

"I don't know. He hit me. I was falling and I saw him grab her by the hair." She was trying to sit up.

"Lowery, can you call Dennis Watts? Tell him to get out here right away?" She nodded. He rose and unclipped his gun. The door to the intensive care room was the first one on the right. He pushed it open carefully. He heard the voice before he could see inside.

"You come in easy, see the situation 'fore you start shootin'."

He pushed the door open and peered around it. Delphi was sprawled on the bed, skirt hiked to show an expanse of brown thigh. Deother was beside the bed holding an oxygen mask pointed toward Delphi's face. In his other hand he held the butane throw away lighter which Lance had seen upstairs when Deother lit his cigarette. Lance could hear a faint hissing sound.

"You fire off that cannon we all go up," Deother said. "There's ten liters of oxygen per minute coming out of this mask and if it goes up the tank goes up."

He was looking at Delphi. He couldn't tell whether or not she was breathing.

"Now me," Deother said, "I got nothin' to lose. You killed Dr. King you killed me, mother fucker. Only man ever gonna do anything for me and you killed him."

"He chose his own way," Lance said carefully, trying not to show the true panic he felt. He'd lost one woman to a madman. He could not afford, for the sake of his sanity, to lose another. "He ran in front of that truck deliberately."

"After you hassle him."

"He was a sick man," Lance said. "We wanted to help him."

"Like you want to help me?"

"Yes, we'll help, Deother. Turn that thing off. Come with me and you'll be treated fairly."

"Right into Central Prison," Deother said. "Well, up yours, motha."

"If Delphi's hurt she needs a doctor," Lance said. "Don't make it worse than it is, Deother. Don't make it four murders."

"Three or four or five, what's the difference? I lose anyway. Now here's what you're going to do, Lance. You're gonna go out there and you're gonna get on the telephone and you're going to call that honky buddy of yours, that Dennis Watts has that airplane. You're gonna get him out at the airport and then you're gonna give me a car and I'm gonna get on that airplane and go to Cuba. You dig that, man?"

"I don't think the plane can fly that far," Lance said, "but we can work something out. Just turn off that oxygen before you blow us all up."

"You think I'm stupid?" Deother snarled. "Think I don't look at things in advance? I had it going good. Dr. King was gonna pay my way, use his influence to get me into a school. All's I had to do was get him a little stuff now and then."

"It was you moved Miss Powers' body and did the other stuff?" Lance asked, his mind working and seeing no way out.

"That don't matter now. Quit stalling."

"But it was you?"

"Yeah, damnit, it was me. Had to get stuff for the man. Did those things to get people away from the medicine chests."

"And you killed her and Burt and Dodo?"

"I'm gonna tell you and then you're gonna move your ass, hear?"

"I hear."

"She saw the damned fool honkey shoot up three caps of Benadryl in the bathroom in her room. Didn't even have enough sense to close the door. Thought she had gone to sleep. She told me to tell the nurses about it. Hell, man, I wasn't gonna let no shriveled-up white honkey woman blow my big chance."

"And Burt and Dodo?" Lance asked. "They walk in on you in the lab?"

"Yeah, well, I had to deal it out to him a little at a time and I had the last of it hidden in there. Stupid honks, letting an orderly give them a shot, served them right."

"You used the epinephrine on them, too?" Lance asked.

"I been doin' some studyin'. I knows about them things." He flourished the lighter. "Now chit-chat time is over, baby. Now you move your ass or you're gonna get it blown off. This tank goes the other one goes and your fox here be right in the middle."

"You'll go too, Deother. Is being alive better?"

"Not in no Central Prison. You get Watts moving and get me your car right around front. Drive it up on the lawn and then you come tell me it's ready. And I don't wanta see no gun."

"All right," Lance said. "But I want to tell you this, brother. You hurt that girl Cuba won't be big enough for you. I'll follow you right into downtown Havana and cut your jewels out before I stuff them down your throat."

"You scarin' the shit out of me," Deother said. "Now you move."

Lance backed away and let the door close. His heart threatened to come out of his chest. Lowery was standing up the hall. He went to her and whispered, "You call Dennis?"

"He's on his way. Del all right?"

"So far. Now I want you to take the keys to my car and go outside and pull it right up in front of the door. When you do that, you go around back and stay there."

"You're going to let him go?" she asked.

"We may have to. He's got nothing to lose. He's got Del."

He half pushed Lowery out the front door and stood there for a minute holding the heavy door open until she had started his car. It was then he heard, from the back side of the hospital, the distant wail of a siren. Watts was coming and he was coming in full cry. Within minutes Deother would hear it, too, as it approached the hospital from the rear. He ran back into the hall, frantically looking for a way out. If there were any human way to prevent it, he would not allow Deother Robinson to leave the hospital with Del as a hostage.

A large foam fire extinguisher was hanging on the wall below a breakable alarm box. He heard the approaching siren at about the same time Deother yelled from inside the intensive care room.

"Lance, you out there?"

"I'm here," Lance called back. "The car is ready."

"What are you trying to pull, you bastard. You think I can't hear?"

The sound of the siren was louder and must have been louder still in the room where Deother stood with the spewing oxygen tank, since there were windows behind him.

"Dennis is on his way to the airport to get the plane ready," Lance yelled. "That's just another car coming to escort you out there, to be sure no one gets in your way."

As he talked, he took the fire extinguisher down off the wall. Standard. Break the seal and press the handle. He positioned himself in front of the door. Like the door to the operating room, it was a swinging door to allow easy entry by stretcher.

"Lance."

"I'm here."

"All right. When I come out of here I'm gonna have a knife right against Delphi's throat. Just remember you can't do nothin' to me fast enough to keep me from getting the carotid. They can't do nothin' 'bout that even in a hospital. You dig?"

"I dig." Lance yelled back, bracing himself, nozzle of the fire extinguisher ready, hand clenched over the handle. It had to be now. He could stop him now or not at all. He wouldn't be able to risk anything with a knife at Del's throat. He took a deep, shuddering breath, lifted his foot, kicked and stepped forward, squeezing even as the door flew back on its hinges and crashed against the stop. The lance of foam caught Deother square in the chest and Lance began spraying the hand holding the lighter. Lance moved forward, drowning the lighter and the hand and then turning the foam straight into Deother's face. Deother's hand came up to protect his face, and Lance threw the entire fire extinguisher. Deother slipped or fell and the tank went over his head to crash glass in the window and fall to bounce off Deother's back. Then Lance was diving over Delphi, over the bed, arms out to encircle Deother, who was getting to his feet.

Lance's chin connected with Deother's shoulder and once again the stars exploded and he was falling, falling, hitting the floor hard and feeling a dull sudden pain as Deother's foot kicked him in the side. He grappled for the leg, gasping, caught it and pulled. Deother came down and went crawling, slipping in the foam. Lance brushed at his eyes and tried to stand. Deother was on his feet now, yelling, wiping at his face. Lance tottered to his feet, trying to make his hand obey orders, to reach for the gun, but Deother was gone, running out the door.

Lance saw him turn the corner and, trying to see around the white flares in his eyes, ran drunkenly after him. As Lance rounded the corner Deother was halfway down the hall, sprinting. The hall was empty. Then the back door burst open and Dennis Watts was there. Deother skidded to a halt and whipped into the door of the lab, closing it behind him.

Dennis met Lance outside the door, gun at the ready. "Is he armed?"

"A knife, maybe," Lance said, almost able to see without white flares.

"Deother, you know there are two of us out here," Dennis said loudly and calmly. "Just come on out with your hands over your head." There was a sound of breaking glass from inside P.J. Charlie's lab. Then silence.

"Are you coming out or do we come in and get you?" Dennis yelled.

After a moment of silence—"Yeah, O.K. I comin' out."

"Just do it easy," Dennis said. "Hands over your head and you won't get hurt."

"Yeah, O.K." Deother said.

Lance had failed twice to stop him. He knew his quickness, his surprising strength. He crouched in the classic ready position, gun held in both hands.

"If that motha tries anything—"

The door opened inward into darkness. Out of the darkness Deother walked slowly, hands clasped on the top of his head. Dennis moved quickly behind him, jerked the arms down, put on handcuffs.

"I'll be back," Lance said, turning to run up the hall, around the corner. Lowery was coming in the front door. She followed him into the intensive care unit. Delphi was sitting up, hand touching her face gingerly. Lance halted just inside the door, breathing hard, wanting to yell or do something. Lowery moved past him and slipped in the foam, righted herself and put her hands on Del's shoulders.

"Are you all right?" Lowery asked.

"My teeth hurt," Delphi said.

Lance heard himself laughing. Lowery looked at him sternly, but she said nothing, knowing that it was, for Lance, a release. He forced himself to stop.

"You take good care of that girl, Lowery," he said.

Dennis was pushing Deother toward the front door. He got in the back seat with Deother. Lance got behind the wheel and backed off the sidewalk and lawn. He put on the blinkers and headed toward the jail. The cell where Burt Scoggins had enjoyed his last party would hold Deother until they could move him to the new jail at Swansey.

It wasn't until Deother spewed vomit, splashing it off the back of the seat, down Lance's neck and onto Dennis' uniform that either of them suspected that Deother, like Burt, had had a taste of the evidence. In Deother's case it was almost half a pint of epinephrine in a ten percent solution.

Chapter Thirteen

If a man is right and knows he's right and fights hard enough for it he sometimes, not always, but sometimes, wins. Jug allowed himself a fresh cut of chewing tobacco and leaned back as the last few precincts, too small to change his narrow victory, begun to come in. It was hotter than hell in the court room where they were tabulating the primary votes, but Jug wasn't feeling the heat. He'd been feeling a different kind of heat for the past few weeks and now it was, somehow, right comfortable.

Now that it was all over he didn't feel shamed by the fact that he'd had some pretty solid opposition. As a matter of fact, he felt better than he'd felt in a long time and part of it was in knowing that he'd been in a fight and had won. Contrary to his expectations, winning a close election was even more satisfying than winning a no contest affair.

But this one would be his last one, one way or the other. At his age there were a lot of things that could happen to end the term before the legal four years ran out, and if he came through the term he'd be pushing seventy so hard that there'd be no question about retirement. That hammock out in the back yard would be his office.

There was a new sense of challenge, too. The county was fractured by the hospital dispute. There was even talk along the eastern areas in particular about petitioning the Legislature to split the county in half and make two counties out of it, cutting the western hardheads adrift to go it on their own. They wanted power, let them have it, some people were saying. Jug figured he'd have to fight that idea quietly. The hospital looked safe, although the new hospital out in the county was being funded. Marian Powers' money would make Bellamy self-supporting, and although the will wasn't probated yet, even the hardest of the Swansey hardheads knew they were not going to close Bellamy. Now they were beginning to talk about splitting up the county government complex, moving part or all of it out into the so-called "central location," which always translated to mean "nearer Swansey."

It would be an interesting four years and as the senior elected official in Clarendon County he'd be right in the thick of it. Well, having a few worries and being active might just keep him alive.

Now that it was over and it was evident that he couldn't be defeated by the few remaining precincts which were slow in reporting, he was being congratulated, even by the young lawyers. He pressed flesh and spat tobacco juice and acted as if he'd had no doubts all along. He even cracked a little joke to the Republican alderman about missing ole Burt because he threw such good parties in the jail. He went around and exchanged well-dones with the other successful primary candidates and then, seeing his chance, snuck off.

He knew Bessie would be on pins and needles, so he went into the judge's chambers and called her and told her she'd have to put up with late-night telephone calls for four more years, barring a miracle and a Republican win in the general election, and then Lance Carver was there when he went back out.

"I can't tell whether you're happy about it or not," Lance said.

"Got mixed emotions, boy." He spat into a brass spittoon in front of the bench. "Guess you got a job for the next four years after all, you want it."

"I got nothing else to do," Lance said.

"Haven't taken time, I reckon, to tell you you did a good job out there at the hospital," Jug said.

"Yeah, well." But he couldn't forget how he'd almost blown it, twice.

"That little gal doin' all right, is she?"

"She's fine. Has to wear braces until a couple of loose teeth tighten up again."

"Pretty little thing," Jug said. "You think so?"

"Very pretty." He put on his hat. "Well, I'm gonna call it a night."

He had seen her twice since that night. She had been polite and smiling, but he kept remembering how he'd risked her life, going into the room giving Deother a chance to light the lighter and blow them all over that wing of the hospital. He couldn't live with that, thinking of it, and then he had made his decision. Never again would he put himself into the position he'd already been in twice. Never again would he let a woman love him, because he seemed to attract nuts and every time a nut came at him a girl got in the way, and he wasn't going to be responsible for that.

He went home and put on a record and turned it down low, drank a beer slowly, smoked while letting the sounds soak in the darkness of his bedroom, lying naked atop the sheets. He just sort of put his mind in neutral and let the song take over. Then he was jarred by the telephone. He found it on the first try in the darkness.

"Lance? This is Del."

"Yeah, hi, Del."

"Listen, it's no big thing, nothing to get excited about, but we have this little situation here at the hospital and we need you to come out."

"What is it?" Lance demanded, sitting up.

"No big deal," she said. "Just drop on by, huh?"

"Be right there." He dressed hurriedly, spun tires getting away, ripped to a stop in the nurse's parking lot out front and ran in. Delphi and Lowery were sitting calmly at the nurse's station, Lowery with her knitting.

Lance stood looking down at her smooth face. There was a twinkle in her eye. "What's happening?" he asked.

"Tell him, Lowery," Delphi said.

"Not a chance," Lowery said. "You tell him."

"All right, all right," Lance said.

"Someone has robbed the sperm bank," Delphi said with a straight face.

"Whaat?"

"The sperm bank. You know, for artificial insemination? They've robbed it and we've received a telephoned threat."

Lance took it hook, line and sinker. "You'd better tell me all about it," he said seriously.

"Well, this male voice, on the telephone?"

"Yes, yes," Lance said impatiently.

"He said he had all the sperms, quarts and quarts of it, and that he was going to wait until the public swimming pool was full of girls and dump it in—"

"And the temperature of that swimming pool water is right at body temperature," Lowery put in.

"—and impregnant every girl in town," Delphi said.

Lowery exploded into laughter behind her hands. Del looked up at him, a bit uncertainly, as he felt first quick anger and then joined Lowery in laughter.

"Shush," Del said. "This is serious."

"Shameless twit," Lance said. He reached down and took her hand. "Maybe you'd better show me the scene of the crime."

"It's that way," she protested, as he led her down toward the patient wing. But she followed and when he found the empty room and thrust her inside she turned her back to him to stare out at the blackness outside the window. "I'm sorry, Lance. I just—"

"Wanted to see me?" he asked.

"Y—yes."

He turned her to face him. She was so tiny, so beautiful. He had to bend his neck to meet her lips. When he broke the kiss she whispered, "I know you were hurt, Lance, and I think I understand. Don't let me force you—"

"There are times to talk and times to shut up," he said, closing her mouth with his.

And later, "I'm not shameless. It's just that you were very carefully staying away—"

"Hush."

"I've got to get back on the floor."

"In a minute. Don't talk. You'll have all day tomorrow to talk. We'll go to the beach."

"I haven't been to the beach all ye—"

Once again he hushed her.

PREFERRED CUSTOMERS!

Leisure Books and Love Spell
proudly present
a brand-new catalogue and a
TOLL-FREE NUMBER

STARTING JUNE 1, 1995
CALL 1-800-481-9191
between 2:00 and 10:00 p.m.
(Eastern Time)
Monday Through Friday

GET A FREE CATALOGUE
AND ORDER BOOKS USING
VISA AND MASTERCARD

LEISURE BOOKS   **LOVE SPELL**